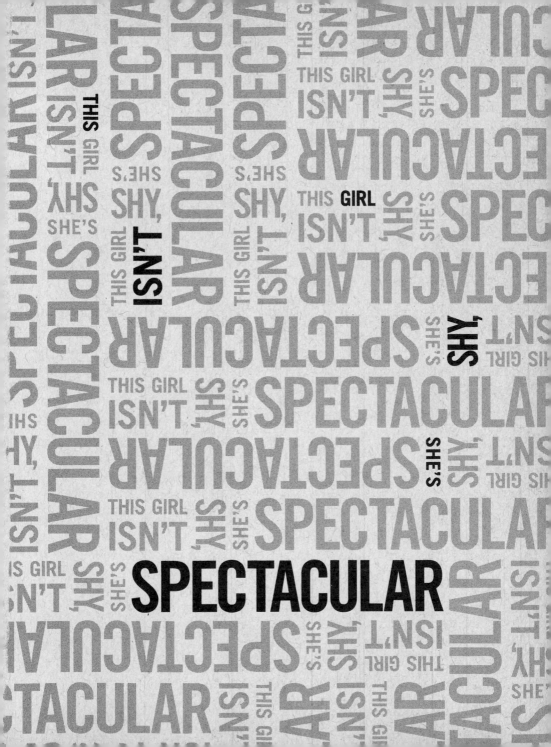

ALSO BY NINA BECK

This Book Isn't Fat, It's Fabulous

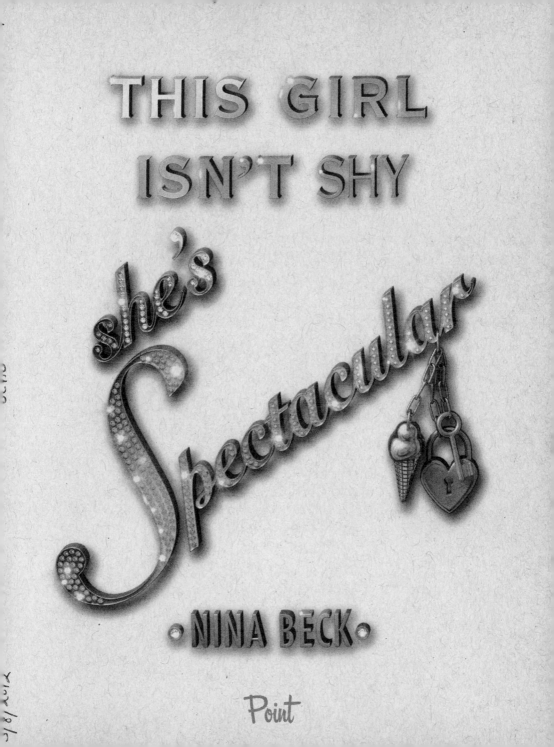

All rights reserved. Published by Point, an imprint of Scholastic Inc., *Publishers since 1920*. SCHOLASTIC, POINT, and associated logos are trademarks and/or registered trademarks of Scholastic Inc.

Library of Congress Cataloging-in-Publication Data
Available

ISBN-13: 978-0-545-01705-3
ISBN-10: 0-545-01705-X

12 11 10 9 8 7 6 5 4 3 2 1   9 10 11 12 13 14/0

Printed in the U.S.A.
First edition, October 2009

Book design by Christopher Stengel and Yaffa Jaskoll

For Eric, Michael, Ted, and Chris,
who make and keep me sane.

Samantha Owens Diary, Age 8

I just read <u>Apples & Oranges</u> and it is the best book I have ever ever ever ever read. Ever.

Samantha Owens Diary, Age 12

Just found out that Pete Bryant will be talking about his book <u>Apples & Oranges</u> at the public library!

Samantha Owens Diary, Age 12

Told Pete Bryant that I wanted to be a writer too. He told me to work really hard and that it would happen. Pete Bryant thinks I'm going to be a writer.

Samantha Owens Diary, Age 15

Pete Bryant is the head of the creative writing program at UCLA. I will do anything to go there. ANYTHING. Mom looked at me like I was crazy but Dad was supportive. Writers stick together, he said. That made me smile. But he said it would be a lot of hard work — but I already know that. But it's going to be perfect. I'm going to be perfect.

UNIVERSITY OF CALIFORNIA, LOS ANGELES

Dear Ms. Samantha Owens:

The admissions committee at University of California, Los Angeles would like to congratulate you on your outstanding academic record. Rarely do we see a student with so much drive to succeed, which is why we're happy to offer you a place in next year's class at UCLA.

Your application indicated that you were applying to the Creative Writing program, and as you know, admission to that program is highly competitive and not guaranteed based on your acceptance to the University at large.

In order to hold your place here . . .

CREATIVE WRITING PROGRAM
UNIVERSITY OF CALIFORNIA,
LOS ANGELES

Dear Samantha,

   Thank you for applying to the Creative Writing program. We were impressed with your academic record (and, dare I say, your perfect attendance record) and eagerly read your writing sample, *The Girl with No Face.*

   I must admit that I was disappointed. While I found your technical writing skills to be above average, I felt that there was a certain amount of passion missing from the sample. Usually I would just dismiss this, but your application essay was filled with exactly the sort of energy I was looking for from your creative writing. If I can make a few suggestions, I'd suggest that you use more of your own personal experiences as a basis for a sample. Right now the character lives a very safe, very boring life and we felt very safe and very bored while reading it.

   While I'm unable to offer you a spot in this year's class, I hope you'll reapply. I see a lot of raw talent in these pages that with just the right story would really shine.

                         Sincerely,
                         Pete Bryant

Michael D. Hammond Journal, Age 8

I want to be a rock star.

Michael D. Hammond Journal, Age 12

I want to be a rock star and kiss
pretty girls.

Michael D. Hammond Journal, Age 13

I want to go live with Mom and be
a rock star in London!

THE UNIVERSITY OF CHICAGO

Dear Mr. Michael D. Hammond III:

We still have not received your application to the University of Chicago, and while it is nothing but a formality, we need confirmation of your interest in attending the University of Chicago.

Your father's position as an alumnus of the University of Chicago and his very active participation in our school's community . . .

THE GIRL WITHOUT
A PERSONALITY

The first three years of high school at the all-girls New Horizons had made it easy for Samantha Owens to be perfect.

The classes were interesting enough, but the best part was that there was absolutely nothing there to distract Sam from her perfect grades, her perfect behavior, and her perfect attendance record. That is, until a girl named Riley Swain showed up and made Sam feel like there was so much she was missing by trying to be "perfect." So, when Sam had received this rejection letter . . . where her idol told her that her story lacked passion and that she should try writing from experience (ugh! She did . . . her sample could have been an autobiography!), she didn't lose hope. She *would* get into the program, she would write a new sample, an even better sample . . . and she would stop trying to be perfect — it didn't serve her nearly as well as she had hoped it would.

So, Sam had called her parents and told them she wanted to come home — and they were so excited, they picked her up the next weekend. New Horizons was a school with a specialized program for teens who were overweight or had eating disorders, but Samantha had never been either since freshman year. Her mother called it "baby fat" and often asked Sam if she wanted to come home, but by then Sam didn't want to leave the friends she'd made at NH. Nor, if she were to be honest, did she want to give up the safety of the school she had become used to.

Now that she realized that safety = boring, she wanted to hit her head against the white wooden desk she sat at in her old bedroom in New York City. Instead she pulled out her notebook and began creating a list. She had tacked the rejection letter from the writing program to the wall above her desk. Sam chewed on the cap of her pen while she studied the signature of her (once) idol, Pete Bryant.

She shook her head sharply and then bent over her notebook and wrote, in her perfect scrawl, *Things I Have Not Done.*

Sam heard a knock at her door and she quickly tore the list out of her notebook, folded it in quarters, and stuck it in her back pocket while calling to either one of her parents to come in.

Sam's mother peeked her head in around the door. "Can I come in?"

"Absolutely," Sam said, turning around in her chair as her mother walked into her room. Sam's mother was beautiful; she had red hair like Sam, but her mother's was a darker shade and she didn't suffer from freckles the way Sam did. She was elegant and nice and everyone who met her — from the guy at the grocery store on the corner of their block to the nurse at the doctor's office — thought Sam's mother was charming.

Sam's mother stood in the middle of the room, looking around, grimacing. Sam followed her line of vision and took in the pink walls with light purple paw prints stamped onto the wall, the fluffy curtains, and the pink-striped bedspread. Things that were absolutely perfect for eighth-grade Sam but that as a senior in high school just didn't work.

"It never bothered me before, because I spent most of my time at school," Sam said.

"Well, now that you're home again" — Sam's mother shot her a brilliant smile — "we should really do something about this."

"I'm only home for a few more months," Sam said, turning back around in her chair. It was like her mother refused to believe that she was attending college. She looked up at the rejection letter above her desk and sighed.

"Sam," her mother said, walking up behind her, her eyes fixed on the rejection letter. "I know you're really disappointed."

"No, it's fine."

"Sam, you've been talking about this school for years. You've been talking about Pete Bryant since you were little."

"Well, that's fine," Sam said, not knowing what to say. She felt like crying. She was overwhelmed by the idea that she had tried as hard as she could and it wasn't good enough.

"Everyone makes mistakes," Sam's mother said.

"I didn't make a mistake, Mom. I want to go there. I want to write."

"I mean him, sweetheart."

"Oh," Sam said.

"So you still want to go, you still want to reapply?" Sam's mother sounded both happy and sad.

"Yes, I'm going to write a new sample and see if they won't reconsider. If that doesn't work . . ."

She didn't want to say it, but she knew what it meant. Going somewhere else for at least a semester and then reapplying, with no assurances that she would ever get in. Sam's mother leaned over and gave Sam a kiss on the forehead and then, with a quick hair ruffle, left her alone with her thoughts.

Sam pulled out the list and added: *I never got into the writing program at UCLA.*

This was the year that Samantha would do everything she hadn't gotten around to in the past three years of being Miss Perfect. This was the year that Samantha would figure out who she was. And then get everything she wanted.

THE BOY WITHOUT
A PLAN

Later that same night, or rather in the morning, Michael D. Hammond III ("D" for short) was returning to his Upper East Side apartment, or rather crawling back to it, with a girl who was very, very intoxicated.

She (because D still couldn't remember what her name was . . . Allison? Amy? Cleo?) had him trapped against the limestone face of his apartment building, while the doorman just inside the double doors did his best to avert his eyes, which was hard to do when Allison-Amy-Cleo was trying to have sex with D right there on the sidewalk. Thankfully it was a cold night out, and there weren't a lot of passersby.

"Sweetheart," D said, in the droll way that he had.

"Ohhhhhh! Did I ever mention how hot your accent is?" she asked, lifting her head from the crook of his neck.

D chuckled; she was an idiot.

"Yes, sweetheart, you mentioned it."

"It makes me want to just eat you up!" And with that, she turned her head and bit his shoulder. Quite hard, or hard enough that D yelped a little — in a very unmasculine way — and had to hold AAC away from him, his hands on her shoulders lest she want to take another bite.

She growled at him, in a way that was obviously something she thought was sexy, but the sight she made: disheveled, her hair everywhere, her eyeliner smeared into dark bruiselike circles under her eyes, and just a hint of red lipstick (more on her teeth than on her lips) (and damn, it would be on his shirt) made the sexy image quite impossible. He wondered about rabies shots.

D sighed. When did this start getting old?

"Why don't you invite me up?" AAC asked, reaching out a finger and dragging it lazily down the front of D's shirt.

D watched the red nail run down the front of his white tailored shirt until it hit his belt buckle, and linger there meaningfully until D removed it and looked at AAC.

"I don't think that's a good idea, darling."

AAC, who had been aiming for Best Sexpot Under 21 five minutes ago, quickly shifted from a mewling face to an angry one. "You're going to just leave me out here? You brought me all the way uptown? For what?"

And because she was about to make a real scene, one that D was sure his father would hear about, and because she was right — she was far away from home and more than a little drunk, who knew what she'd do to a poor hapless cabdriver if he let her go like this? — he nodded.

"You're right, I apologize for being thoughtless. Would you please accompany me upstairs? I'll make us some coffee and then call you a car."

"Coffee, eh?" she said, smiling again, and pulling out her compact from her bag and checking her makeup. She must have been drunker than D realized, because she squinted into the mirror, smiled broadly at her reflection, and then snapped it shut again. "I'd love to, Michael."

"Call me D," he said.

"D," she said, then giggled, then snorted. D walked her inside, the doorman opening the door, shooting him a smirky glance. D nodded as he practically dragged her by the arm past the concierge's marble desk and toward the elevator. When he got her into it, she slumped lazily against the wall.

"Will I meet your parents?"

"Hardly," D said, trying to check his collar for red lipstick.

"You don't want me to meet your parents?" AAC wailed, life flowing back into her.

"Of course I do," D said, standing there as he adjusted his collar in the blurry reflection of the back of the elevator doors. "It's just that they are hardly ever here and if they were, I could hardly introduce you."

For some reason, whether she misunderstood or didn't hear, AAC nodded and smiled at D, wrapping her arms around him. D pushed her hands away gently, but they just kept coming! It was like the girl was an octopus. D made a mental note not to leave any more parties with drunk girls.

It's just that AAC hadn't appeared nearly so drunk (or messy) at the party. D made another mental note not to drink so much himself, or at least not let himself get so sober so quickly after leaving.

The elevator opened up into the penthouse apartment and D walked across the foyer as AAC followed, slower, oohing and aahing about the place that D mostly enjoyed alone — his father having another apartment of his own several blocks away. AAC dropped into the settee in the middle of the foyer as D pulled out his phone to call for a car.

"How do you take your coffee?" D asked, turning back toward AAC, who had already fallen asleep on the settee.

"Of course," he said. "Probably better this way." He walked into the kitchen and grabbed a bottle of water from the fridge and, untwisting the cap, slammed the fridge shut with the back of his foot as he turned to walk away.

D guzzled his water as he walked back into the foyer, and then, spotting a drooling AAC, walked past her into his bedroom. He checked his text messages and then sent one to his best friend, Riley Swain.

I will never drink again.

Two minutes later he received a text back that said:

You're drunk or you would never make such a ridiculous claim.

He wrote back:

Duly noted.

Just as he was putting away his cell, AAC stumbled into his room, mumbling D's name under her breath. She sat, in the middle of the floor, and D — perhaps not for the first time that night — felt a little ashamed and really annoyed at himself for what he had let his life become.

"Is this your room?" she asked. She looked up at him, tilted her head, and then lurched over and threw up. D jumped back, barely avoiding the projectile vomit. "Can I call you Michael?"

"No," D said, looking at the mess AAC had made on his floor.

D picked up his phone again, dialed, and then said into the receiver, "I need to cancel that car, but have it here at seven A.M." Then he carried AAC into a spare bedroom to sleep it off. When she was comfortably situated, still fully clothed, she fell into a deep, still sleep and began snoring. Loudly.

That left D alone with the mess that was his life and the mess that was his rug. He had to clean up both, all on his own.

He let this sink in as he cleaned up the rug the best he could, then jumped into the shower. When he was done, he drank another bottle of water and sat at the desk in the living

9

room. On the desk there were two piles. One was several inches high, a pile of applications that had not yet been filled out. The other was just two sheets of paper, an acceptance letter from his father's alma mater and a note from his father's secretary saying that he needed to sign the forms she had already filled out for him and send them back to her.

D picked up the acceptance letter and crumpled it in his hands. He didn't want the life his father offered, but never made an attempt to have a different life. His father had called him to his study a few weeks ago and told him that he needed to do *something*, and if he couldn't figure it out on his own — he would be happy to figure it out for D.

D could hear AAC's snores reverberating through the apartment and, with a slight shake of the head, decided that he'd had enough of screwing up his life. He'd try; he'd be better. He'd fix things.

He pulled a sheet of paper out of the drawer and began writing a list of all the things he'd done in the past four years that were messing up his life, one mistake at a time. His eye on the applications, he swore he wouldn't get involved with any more girls until he finished those applications and told his father that he wouldn't be attending his school.

This was the year that D would figure out what he was really made of. And didn't do anything he wanted to do.

#1 TRY TO CHANGE

Samantha sat right on the edge of Central Park, facing Columbus Circle. She had texted Riley to let her know she was sitting "behind the big monument thing" and she began people watching. People were rushing across the walkway; nobody but Samantha was really sitting, probably because it was too chilly in late January to be sitting outside in the middle of Manhattan. But there she was.

She watched the cabdrivers fly around the circle and listened as couples chatted on their way to the Time Warner Center.

She loved the park — she didn't even mind the city that surrounded it.

Riley walked up next to Sam and kicked her shoe lightly with her own. "I'm not going to even tell you how difficult it was to get here! I had to take *the subway*!"

Sam faked a little gasp that made Riley purse her lips. Sam always admired the way that Riley held herself. She was her own person and never really cared what others thought about her. At least that's the impression she gave off. She was pretty, but Sam knew it was her personality that really attracted everyone around her. It was very much "I am who I am, and you'll love me anyway."

Sam wished she were more like that. Sam even wished she had Riley's sense of fashion — like today, for instance, Riley was wearing a long black Anne coat, with two overlarge buttons keeping it closed at her chest; it had a childlike look to it, but coupled with perfect 1950s-style makeup and knee-high boots, she looked like she just stepped out of a magazine. Sam sighed at her own jeans and bubble jacket, but stood up and walked with her toward the shopping center and up to the second-floor bookstore anyway.

"I haven't had a café latte in, like, forever," Riley said as they stood in line together. "But then I lost four pounds."

"That's great?" Sam said.

"No, I think I only lost it in my bazongas, which means none of my bras feel right, and so I need to gain it back," Riley said, ordering a café latte and pointing at a muffin behind the glass. The girl behind the counter placed this next to Sam's tea and rang them up together. Riley waved away Sam's money when she took out her wallet.

"You know," Sam said, carrying her tea away from the counter and spotting a table in the cramped little café space, "you could always think of it as a reason to buy new clothes."

Riley stopped with the muffin halfway to her mouth. "Damn, you're right." She put the muffin down. "Did they teach you that at NH? I don't remember that."

"They didn't exactly tie in healthy eating habits with new clothing, no. But they said a lot of 'Eat a balanced diet of healthy food, blah, blah, blah.'"

"But I want a muffin!" Riley cried, looking sadly at her now-untouched muffin.

"You don't have to be perfect. Just try to eat better on a regular basis," Sam said.

"You don't have to be perfect?" Riley asked. "My Sam is saying you don't have to be perfect?"

Sam frowned. "Yeah, that's kinda what I wanted to talk to you about."

"Muffins?"

"No, being perfect."

"Yes, well, it is very difficult," Riley said, fluffing her hair. Sam smiled at her friend.

"I want to be less perfect," Sam said.

"Well, wearing those sneakers and jeans is a really good start," Riley said.

"Ha-ha," Sam said, then stuck out her tongue at Riley. "I didn't get into the UCLA writing program."

Riley dropped her muffin. "What? But your grades . . . your extracurriculars . . . they were . . ."

"Perfect," Sam finished for her. "The problem was, my writing sample wasn't."

"But I read it and thought it was great."

"Well," Sam said, looking into her cup of tea, "apparently they thought differently. They said it lacked personality."

"What? What does that mean?"

"It means they want me to write something from experience, something more *me*, so that I can make it more exciting."

"But that sample, that character, *was* you."

Samantha flinched.

"I mean . . ."

"No, no, it's OK. I understand exactly what you mean," Sam said, taking a deep breath. "Which is why I need your help."

Riley paused, motioning for Sam to continue.

"I made a list of things that I haven't done in the past four years, things I want to do this year . . . and some of it I can't . . ."

"Of course I'll help!" Riley said, bouncing up and down in her seat. "This is going to be so great! What's on the list? Can I see the list? Is a haircut on the list, because that would be so perfect . . . I mean, so wonderful!"

Samantha touched her hair, which was pulled back into a big puffy ponytail at the back of her head. "Um, well, number one is that I tried to never change, and so I guess . . ."

Riley took a deep breath. "Makeover?"

Sam nodded slightly.

Riley's face broke into a deep, deep grin, and she grabbed Samantha's hand from across the table. "This will be so perfect."

"That's what I'm afraid of."

Two hours later, Riley was standing behind Samantha's chair in a very posh salon called, ironically, The Salon. It was on the Upper West Side and looked like nothing special from the outside of the building, but Riley swore by it. She also had to swear a lot to get them inside of it, because the receptionist kept standing by the fact that they were completely booked up until March.

Riley had said a few choice words (Black AmEx were two of them) that had the receptionist put her on hold, and a few minutes later she asked the fabulous Ms. Swain to stop by with her friend at their earliest convenience.

Riley had introduced Samantha to her "favorite hairdresser ever," a short, skinny man who called himself Eduardo, who — Samantha had noticed — had the worst fake accent ever. Plus, Sam was pretty sure she heard one of the hair washers call him Eddie.

"I'm thinking a little more Katie Holmes and a little less Posh Spice," Riley said, speaking as if Samantha weren't even there.

"Katie Spice?" Eduardo said with a strangely mixed accent that was a quarter Spanish, three-quarters Queens, and just a hint of fake British on top. "I love it. I do it!"

"Yay!" Riley cried, smiling at him in the mirror, fluffing Samantha's red hair from behind, making it puffier and frizzier than it already was.

"My hair won't do that," Sam said, staring at herself in the large mirror. She looked like a disembodied head in the large black gown that was tied up around her chin. A big disembodied head with a rat's nest of red hair on top of it.

"Eduardo can make hair do anything," Riley assured her. Eduardo nodded in agreement as he began plugging in an assortment of dryers, curlers, irons, and electric razors.

"I will make you into the Mona Lisa," Eduardo said.

"The Mona Lisa had *long* hair," Samantha said hopefully.

"And a really wide jaw," Riley said, blowing her bangs out of her eyes.

"You've got such a sweet face," Eduardo said, grasping her chin in his fingers to turn it this way and that. "A short haircut really complements."

"And 'shorter' really means cutting almost eight inches of hair off the back of my head?" Sam whined. "It took me almost twelve years to get it this long. I never cut it."

Riley made a face and Samantha looked at herself hard in the mirror.

Samantha kept staring, hoping perhaps for a revelation to make itself known. Like God would set a bush on fire so that it could tell her exactly what to do. The only thing close to a burning bush was the big frizzy mess of hair that Eduardo was currently trying to tame with a hair pick.

"Cut it," Sam decided. "Do it, fast, before I can change my mind."

"Eduardo!" Riley cried, and then moved to hold Sam's hand.

Eduardo pulled all of Sam's hair back from her face, holding it with one hand in a fistful of ponytail, and with one clean cut of his very sharp scissors, off it came.

Twelve years. Eight inches. Samantha felt her eyes well up. Change was painful.

"It's done!" Eduardo yelled, holding the ponytail high above his head. An older, more matronly woman sitting in the chair next to Sam's leaned over and patted Sam's arm, saying, "Good for you."

The rest of the salon clapped; the hair washers hooted as Samantha did her best to blink away her tears and remain smiling. That is, until she looked in the mirror.

Eduardo heard her gasp and quickly turned her chair around. "No, no, darling. Not yet. Not until you're all done." He readjusted her gown while Riley walked away to take a phone call. "It's like — you know — it's like they say . . . 'Don't look down.' It will only scare you. Better to wait."

"But don't people *always* look down?" Sam pointed out.

"Yes, and what does this do?"

"Makes them realize the precariousness of their position and makes them wonder what kind of idiots they were to come to New York months before graduation in a stupid attempt to change their life before it was too late?" she asked, on the verge of a panic attack.

"Mmm-hmm. Exactly." Eduardo patted the top of her head, before jerking her chair back so Sam was lying prone (and terrified), as Eduardo pulled foils out of his apron and began sectioning off Sam's hair and painting them with color.

"Just trust me, *mon cherie*, this will be superb."

Samantha simply nodded and didn't have the heart to tell him that his French was simply awful.

Sam did have to admit that The Salon was wonderful. The hair washers all sat and spoke with her when she was waiting for the hair dye to do its thing, and she loved hearing all the gossip about the place, the way that everyone worked together and seemed to have their lives intertwine. It was a very nice place. The walls were painted a bright orange and there were large mirrors with gilded frames hanging everywhere. It was charming and chic — and Sam had ample time to observe all this as two hours later, she was still in the same chair, but by now Eduardo was using a small hair iron.

It looked like a small set of black tongs, and he was using it to iron out small sections of hair, bit by bit. It let off a gust of steam whenever Eduardo released her hair, which didn't seem to worry anyone but her. She kept trying to signal to Riley, who was too busy telling Eduardo about Eric to note whether Sam's hair was going to fall out from excessive burning.

"It's just that he's so far away and he can only visit once a month!" Riley said to Eduardo. Sam was happy that she didn't have to respond; she had already heard this entire spiel. Twice, each day — ever since Riley returned to Manhattan after having started dating Sam's friend Eric, the son of the New Horizons headmistress.

Sam soon realized that Riley wasn't really complaining, she just needed something to be dramatic over, so Sam let her talk.

"How about you, *mes pétit*?"

Sam cringed at his incorrect French.

"Do you have anyone special?" Eduardo asked her.

Samantha shook her head. There was no one . . . and immediately she heard Pete Bryant's deep voice in her head saying her life (not just her writing) was shy and boring.

"Not yet," Riley said.

"Not yet," Eduardo repeated. "But once the boys see you with this new haircut, they won't be able to keep themselves away. They will be hungry for you!"

Riley nodded, looking up from her phone, where she was probably texting Eric something amazingly sentimental and goofy.

Samantha just smiled at Eduardo.

"Oh, I see," he said. "You don't believe Eduardo. But I tell you. You will fall in love. I know. I'm . . . how do they say . . . ?"

"Psychic," Riley threw out.

"Yes, that's it! I am psychic," Eduardo said, pulling another small section of hair between the iron. "And I predict that this will be the most amazing haircut you've ever had and that you will meet the boy of your dreams."

Samantha did her best to smile politely even though she didn't believe a word Eduardo was saying. Really? A psychic hairdresser?

But he was at least half right: By the time he was finished and had turned her around in her chair to look in the mirror, Samantha had to admit it was the most amazing haircut she had ever had. It was sleek and soft looking, it swished when she shook her head back and forth, and all she wanted to do was touch it over and over again.

"Stop touching it," Eduardo said, shooing her hands away and smoothing it down with something that made it shiny and glisteny.

"My hair is shiny!" Samantha said, pointing in the mirror. Riley rolled her eyes but Eduardo smiled and gave her shoulders a little squeeze.

Riley surveyed the finished style while Samantha smiled at herself in the mirror. "Beautiful work, Eduardo. As usual!" They kissed each other on the cheek, and called each other "darling," as Riley slipped him a tip and left The Salon to make a "few more stops that were necessary to the makeover process."

Samantha took a deep breath to steel herself against the things to come. She knew makeovers were supposed to be fun, so she concentrated on keeping the smile plastered on her face while she ignored the nervous whirl in the pit of her stomach.

D TRIES TO CHANGE TOO, BUT KEEPS THE SAME HAIRCUT

That night, D was lying flat on his back staring at Riley's bedroom ceiling. She had taped a blown-up picture of Eric there, which not only creeped D out a little but severely clashed with the rest of her room.

The rest of her room was done in beautiful shades of beige with a big fluffy white bed in the middle of the room (which was currently littered with empty bags from every large department store in the city). The room seemed at odds with Riley's personality, which was so loud and vibrant, but it actually fit her perfectly if you knew her. It was warm, a touch traditional, and very cozy.

"So you just have to be good?" Riley asked.

"Not just 'be good,' I need to do things *differently*. I have to behave," D said. "And I need your help."

Riley coughed. "I'm not exactly the most well-behaved girl you know."

"I know, but you also know me better than anyone else." D shifted onto one elbow so he could look at her. "Promise me. Promise me you'll keep me on the straight and narrow."

Riley looked at him. "You're serious, aren't you?"

"Dead serious."

Riley thought about it for a moment. "OK, sure. I can do that."

"Really?"

"Of course. Just tell me what you need me to do."

D stood up. "I don't know, help me become someone else?"

Riley laughed. "Um, well, I can try."

"I guess I just need help remembering that I need to stay away from the things in my life that I'm always making bad choices about."

"Like?"

"You know: parties, alcohol, girls."

"You want to give those up?"

"Want to? No. Have to, Riley. Have to. I need to get serious about school. I can't just . . . keep living the life that my father wants me to live . . . I need to be the person I need to be, not the person he needs me to be." D stood and looked around Riley's room, which was still covered in bags and packaging from Samantha's shopping the day before. "Did you go shopping?"

"Actually," Riley said, kneeling on the bed and surveying the mess that was her room, "these aren't mine."

"Likely story."

"No, seriously, I'm helping another friend."

"With Gucci?"

"Is there any better form of help?"

D shrugged. "What did this person need help with?"

"She wanted a life change too."

"Oh? Aren't you little Ms. Life Change Guru lately?"

"Yes, I'm thinking about getting business cards," she said, stepping gingerly onto the floor, weaving her way around the bags, hangers, and open boxes. "Riley Swain, Life Changer."

"That would be an understatement."

D saw Riley smiling at him, but he was distracted: He still wasn't sure what he wanted to do with his life, but he knew that it wasn't right just to go through the motions. He used to have a lot of dreams (OK, so they mostly consisted of becoming a rock star), but lately? Lately, he needed more than dreams, he needed a plan.

"OK, so it'll be my job to keep you away from those bad influences."

"Basically."

"Done!" Riley said. "Now, will you take me out shopping? All these sad, empty bags are making me depressed."

D raised an eyebrow. "Perhaps I should keep *you* away from bad influences."

"D — if I was in any way susceptible to 'bad influences' I'd surely ask for your assistance. Until then, all I need is for you to hold my purse while I try things on and tell me I look absolutely fabulous."

"You can't just use one of the attendants or even a mirror?"

"They lie."

"The attendants or the mirrors?"

"Both. Equally."

"Fine, but I have to be home by five."

"What?" Riley asked, stopping short.

"School starts tomorrow. I thought I might have a quiet dinner and then go to bed."

Riley snorted. D shrugged and then gestured toward the door before following Riley out of the room.

#2 STAY OUT ALL NIGHT

It was the night before her first day at a new school and Samantha knew she would never get to sleep. She sat in her room for most of the evening, full of nervous energy, scribbling in her journal, trying to come up with a good idea for her new writing sample, but the only result was stick figures on the corners of the pages, which only served to add to her frustration.

Her parents had each come in to "tuck her in," as they called it, around eleven. Sam was slightly bemused by the fact that they still thought she was a little kid. But Sam realized that the last time she had had a first day of school at home, she had been closer to seven than seventeen, as she was now. But Sam just hoped they didn't try to walk her to school the next morning.

Figuring she'd never get to sleep before midnight, she flipped open her phone and texted Riley.

#2 on my list: Stay out all night. Any ideas?

Riley texted back right away:

I have the perfect plan.

When Samantha got off the phone, she snuck out of her room and walked down the hall to her brother's room to knock gently on the door.

"Are you decent?" she called.

"Yeah, why are you whispering?"

"Keep your voice down!"

"Nah," Andrew said, opening the door and walking out. "Dad sleeps like the dead, snores too . . . so Mom wears earplugs. You're safe. Just wait until they go to bed."

"Oh."

"Yeah, I forget there are things you would've missed, being away at school all this time." Andrew shucked his hair out of his eyes and sat down in the chair at the desk, and began sifting through the desk drawers. Samantha looked at her brother, who looked more like their dad, while Sam looked like their mom. Andrew had their father's dark hair that fell in curly locks around his eyes, and he had the same baby face. He was a cute kid, average height, and still sorta gangly.

Andrew went to a magnet school in the city — he had left all his friends in middle school to go to a special art and design school in Midtown, but he loved his classes and loved his teachers, so he always said it was worth it.

Samantha wondered if he regretted it — leaving his friends and starting all over at a new school for his freshman year — or rather she wondered if she'd regret leaving all her friends at her old school. . . . Were they more similar than Sam thought?

"So have you ever tried to sneak out?"

"Not really. I mean, once or twice," he said, his head dipping down until his chin rested against his chest. "I used to go see this poet do this spoken word poetry thing."

Samantha stopped. "You snuck out to see poetry?"

Andrew blushed again.

"OK, well, that's cool," she said. "I need to sneak out tonight, I'm meeting Riley."

"Mom and Dad would probably just —"

"That's not the point. I . . . I need to do this," Sam said.

Andrew just nodded, and Sam figured she had a pretty cool brother, especially when he started to explain the trick of sneaking out of the Owens' residence.

"Where are you going anyway?"

"Um, Riley is bringing me to a club."

"You're going to drink?" Andrew perked up. Sam had the sneaking suspicion that her younger brother was a bit of an innocent (much like herself) and wondered if she should lie so he'd think she was cooler.

"Nah, honestly I can't even drink that stuff without making the dumbest faces."

He laughed. "Me too. I drank a beer last year and threw up."

"Ew."

"Yeah, seriously."

"Well, I better get ready. . . ."

"Yeah." Andrew stood up and looked around the room. "I'm glad you're back. I mean, it's nice having my big sister here."

"It's nice being back, Andy."

"Andrew."

"Andrew," she said, nodding and tapping her forehead. "I'll try and remember you're not some little kid anymore."

"Yeah, I guess," he said. "Good night."

He closed the door behind him and Sam saw the light under the door go out before she began changing. Andrew told her that they still checked on him before going to bed themselves, so that's what Sam was waiting for. When she heard the footsteps slow as they passed her door, and saw the light flood through the crack as they peeked in at her, Samantha thought serene thoughts and tried her best to relax her face and breathe steadily. Hopefully they wouldn't hear her heart pounding.

After what felt like a million years, they closed the door behind them and Sam could hear her parents amble down to their bedroom, content that both their children were safely tucked into bed. Samantha kicked off the covers. She didn't bother with the shoes, as per her brother's advice, and instead hooked her fingers into the heels and grabbed her bag, slowly moving her way out of the room and down the hall — being careful not to step in the center of the path, which was more likely "to squeak like hell and get your ass caught."

Once she had the front door of the apartment closed behind her, she took a deep, steadying breath and then bent over to put her shoes on.

Samantha's heart didn't stop racing until she got out of the cab in front of the club, where Riley was waiting for her, wearing something similar to what Sam was wearing: jeans, top, and heels.

"You made it!"

"Of course I did," Samantha said. "Piece of cake." But she still looked nervously over her shoulder, terrified that her parents or someone they knew would spot her and the jig would be up.

"Want to go inside?"

"Absolutely, let's go." Samantha smiled at the guy who stood by the front door, for a second alarmed that she might not be able to get in, but he gave Riley a friendly smile and herself a nod — and for a second, Samantha felt flooded with the coolness of what her life had become. Dangerous, but definitely cool.

D TRIES TO STAY IN ALL NIGHT

D couldn't sleep. It wasn't even eleven and it simply felt unnatural to be lying in bed when he could be out. Now, D realized that he had said he was going to get some rest before school started the next day, but how much rest did one really need? Wouldn't it be worse to oversleep, which would throw off his entire sleep pattern, and he would feel completely ill in the morning?

No, no, instead he should definitely get up and perhaps go for a little stroll until he actually felt tired, and he could still be home before midnight. . . .

And a stroll could mean anything; maybe he should text Riley and see if she wanted to —

No, no, it was only going to be a very short stroll and he didn't want to bother her for no reason. By the time he found her, he'd probably be back in bed, sleeping like a baby. Better just to go out and come back when he was ready, without bothering his best friend. Plus, he could control himself for the evening: no parties, no alcohol, no girls.

How hard could it be?

D pulled on some clothing, grabbed his wallet with his credit cards and fake ID, and headed out the front door, slamming it shut behind him.

#3 DO SOMETHING THAT IS DEFINITELY A BAD IDEA

There weren't nearly as many perfect people as Samantha thought there would be. Hollywood had done her ill. When she pictured the inside of an NYC club, she pictured perfect bodies, clad perfectly in leather or that other weird leathery latex material, all dancing perfectly (if sluttishly) with really, really hot men. In general, Sam thought she was going to walk into a music video, but instead the real club was a much weirder mix. Most of the people there were closer to her own age, so they had to get their hands stamped at the door (hers had a big NO stamped on it), and they milled around the edges, elbowing and jostling one another while a relatively small group danced in the middle in front of a band.

Sam had expected a DJ.

The band was pretty cool; there was a girl jumping and screaming into the mic and a really cute guitarist. Riley elbowed her lightly when she caught Sam staring. Sam blushed and turned away.

"Look, do not pick up any guys here."

"What?"

"Do not pick up any guys here, just enjoy yourself!" Riley yelled over the music as the band started a new set. "I need to use the powder room. Will you be OK here by yourself, or do you want to . . ."

"No, no, I'm fine," Samantha said, blushing again. She really needed to learn to control her blushing — she couldn't even talk about the bathroom without turning a serious shade of pink.

"OK, be right back!" Riley said, then blew a kiss as she walked toward the far corner of the space.

Samantha looked around: the inside of the club . . . bar . . . venue? The inside of the venue was painted black. Everything was black, except the mirror behind the bar on the far right-hand side and the lights on the stage, which were pink and blue and sometimes pulsed with the beat of the drums. It made Sam's pulse race just to watch it. She was so happy she was here.

Except she was standing in the middle of the room all by herself.

In an attempt to occupy herself, Sam decided she needed a soda.

She headed toward the bar, which took much longer than one would expect to cross a simple room, but there were more people going in the opposite direction. When Sam finally made it, she sighed deeply and bent over to call the bartender, only to realize that she was stuck to the bar.

"Oh, gross," she said, peeling herself off.

"Yes, you've got to watch that," said a low voice with a beautiful British accent.

"Yes," Sam said, feeling her cheeks heat up. She looked to her right and the beautiful British accent was matched by a beautiful boy. Samantha flushed again, wondering if it was OK to call a boy beautiful — but if it were in only specific cases, this would be one of them. He was taller than she was, by a few inches at least. He had dark hair that stood out against his pale skin and the most beautiful blue eyes. He was . . . beautiful. She smiled shyly and turned her attention back toward the bartender, who seemed to be having a full-fledged conversation at the other end of the bar and was ignoring everyone else.

"If you're trying to get her attention, I hope you have some time to wait," the boy said, picking up a short glass that was half filled with ice and amber liquid. He did not have a stamp on his hand. Sam wondered how old he was — he certainly didn't look twenty-one, but what did she know?

"Um, do you think I should come back?" Sam asked, her eyes darting between the boy and the bartender.

"Nah, she'll come around eventually," he said, smiling. "Plus, I like the company of beautiful girls."

Samantha wished she were one of those girls who could respond right away, but her immediate reaction was to wonder if he was flirting with her or making fun of her. She decided to take a deep breath and assume it was the former.

"Do you think she'd look over if I reached over the edge and just grabbed the spigot?" Sam asked, pointing toward the soda spigot on the other side of the bar.

"Probably. Do you want to try? I can keep a lookout for you."

Sam giggled. And then stopped. And then giggled again. Because she just realized, she was flirting with this boy, and this beautiful boy was flirting with her, or at least offering to help her do something awfully bad.

"In fact, why don't you just climb over and pour us both a little something," he said, finishing his drink. "I doubt she'd even notice."

Sam laughed and felt adrenaline pulsing through her veins, and suddenly she wanted to. She wanted to hop over the bar and do exactly what the beautiful British boy suggested even though she was sure he meant it all as a joke.

Instead she stood up and walked away — noting his slightly surprised expression — and with a quick glance at him, where he sat with his eyebrows raised, stepped behind the bar.

For a moment she stood there, glancing down at the bartender, who was still completely involved in whatever interesting conversation she was having with a really hot guy. Sam wiped her sweaty palms on her pants and then tucked her hair behind her ears.

"What can I get you?" she asked, approaching the boy from behind the bar.

He laughed, deep and long, and when he was done, his eyes were twinkling and he smiled at her like he had never seen someone like her before and it made Sam want to spend all night across from him, smiling back.

"A Jack and Coke," he said.

Definitely older, Sam thought, feeling slightly disappointed. A little too old for her, even in her current risqué state of mind, but he wasn't too old to flirt with, right? Just too old to . . . well, probably too old to ask for his number. He probably had all kinds of girls his own age asking for his number; he'd never give it to her. She was quiet, and just "OK" looking, and . . .

He looked at her expectantly.

"Oh, the drink," she said. "Um, what's Jack?"

He smiled and stood up in his seat, leaning over the bar pointing toward a tall bottle with a spout shoved into the neck. It had the words JACK DANIELS written on a black label across the front. Of course.

Behind the bar there had to be hundreds of bottles with liquids at varying levels. And glasses. And practically no light by which to see anything. This was definitely not a safe working environment.

Sam picked up the first glass she saw that looked to be of an average size and . . .

"Just put ice in and pour at the same time you pour the soda."

Sam nodded and picked up the bottle, remembering all the movies she'd seen that had scenes that took place in bars. The bartender always spun the bottle around before pouring; Sam wondered if that was to mix the contents and tried to spin the bottle in her hand, but dropped it (and caught it before it hit the floor) and blushed instead.

She couldn't even look up; she was sure the boy (or would he be a man at twenty-one?) — the guy was certainly going to be amused, if not laughing outright.

She poured the drink, only sloshing a little over the edge as she placed it on the counter.

"Oh, wait," she said, picking it up again and placing a little cocktail napkin underneath it.

"Perfection," he said, taking a sip and coughing a little. "A bit strong, but otherwise perfect. I'm impressed."

Sam knew if she blushed one more time she'd never be able to cool off to a normal body temperature again.

"Excuse me?" an irritated voice called from a few seats down at the bar. A man was holding a folded twenty out to her.

"Um?" she said, looking at the man, who obviously wanted service, and then back at the guy, who had begun laughing again.

"Can I get some service?" he said loudly, and for a second Sam worried that the other bartender (cough, the only bartender) would turn around and spot her. She shouldn't have worried.

"Um?" Sam said, unable to form a coherent sentence.

"I want two lemon drops, a Heinie, and a Bass."

He wanted a *heinie*?

Sam repeated the order back to him, while he looked at her like she was an idiot, and said, "Sorry, it's my first night."

The other patron's face softened a little and he said, "Threw you into the deep end, did they?"

Sam nodded.

"And you're not getting much help," he said with a nod toward the other bartender, who was leaning over the top of the bar, clearly not worried about sticking to it, as much as she was worried about . . .

Sam nodded again.

"Two beers, this one and this one," the patron said, pointing toward two beers on tap. And then he walked Sam through how to make the shots (which were surprisingly complicated); he even left her a generous tip as he took the drinks away, but not knowing how much the drinks actually cost (and not actually working there), Sam left it in a small pile behind the counter, tucked behind the pint glasses.

Before she had a chance to think, before she got more than a glance back toward the guy with the fabulous British accent, who was still watching her and smiling, two more drink orders were thrown at her. Thankfully these just necessitated her handing over bottles, and then before anyone else could ask for a drink, she threw up her hands and said she was on a break — and walked back toward the boy.

"That was amazing," he said. "You're amazing."

"I mean, how hard is it to pour a drink?" she asked.

He shook his head. "Amazing."

"Actually, I was wondering . . ." he said, but caught Sam staring over his shoulder at Riley, who was looking around the club for Sam, and looked around too. Sam froze. So did the boy on the other side of the bar. "Bloody hell."

Sam immediately realized that the boy and Riley knew each other. Of course they knew each other! Was there a hot boy within a twenty-mile radius that Riley didn't know? Oh god, did they *know* each other?

"Do you want to get out of here?"

"What?"

"Do you want to get out of here?" he repeated, slower this time.

Sam's list item consisted of doing something that was a bad idea . . . but not crazy. She couldn't (and wouldn't) leave the club with someone she didn't know.

"Um, I don't think that's a good idea. . . ."

He smiled a half smile, a crease appearing in his cheek, and Samantha was struck again by just how beautiful he really was.

"It's definitely not a good idea," he replied, "but my friend is approaching and if she sees me here, she will undoubtedly

40

make my life a living hell, and I'd escape but I don't want to do so without at least getting your number."

"I . . ."

"How about we go find someplace to talk for a minute?"

"What are you doing?" a high, shrill female voice squealed.

"Oh, shit," the boy said, looking to his left, while Samantha looked to her right only to see an angry bartender advancing on her. She yipped, jumped, and ran out from behind the bar as the bartender gave chase. The beautiful boy followed at a more acceptable speed.

Sam ran straight to the girls' bathroom and hid in a stall, tucking her feet up on the seat. There was a soft knock on the door and then an amused British voice asking, "Can I come in?"

"Hell," the boy said as he squeezed himself into the stall with Sam, closing the door behind him. "I haven't been in one of these in a long time."

Sam raised her eyebrows but he just shook off the question.

"Um . . . so can I get your number?" he asked.

"Well," she hedged. "I think you're too old for me."

He shot her a surprised look before his face broke into a smile again. "I'm seventeen."

"You are? But you were . . ." she said, pointing back toward the bar. Not only did she illegally pour drinks but she illegally poured drinks for a minor. Oh, hell.

"Fake ID."

"You need a fake ID?" Samantha asked.

"Well, if I want to drink, I do."

"Oh," she said. It made sense and it didn't. "Do you need to drink?"

"Need to? No. Want to? Yes."

"Oh." Enter an awkward lull in the conversation.

"I think I might be losing my touch," he said.

"What? Why?"

"I asked for your number twice and you don't want to give it to me," he continued before Sam could argue or agree. "But how about this: I'll give you mine. And if you want to talk or go out sometime, you can call me. And then I wouldn't have snuck into the girls' bathroom for no reason."

She opened her mouth and then shut it again. Instead of replying, she took out her phone and punched in the numbers as he rattled them off, but before she hit SEND, he smiled and opened the stall.

"I hope you'll call," he said, over his shoulder. "Good night, then."

"Good night," she said, balancing on top of the toilet.

He nodded and shut the stall door. She smiled and looked down at her phone. Outside the stall, she heard the door open and a loud gasp of a woman.

And then, "I'm sorry, mademoiselle." And the door close again.

Samantha laughed and looked down at her phone: The number was there, but she realized she hadn't asked for his name, so she quickly saved it under "THEBOY." She flipped her phone closed as Riley walked in.

"There you are! I was looking for you. . . ."

Sam smiled and asked if they could go home.

"Oh god," Riley said, looking at Sam. Stepping closer and pulling her face closer to hers so she could inspect her eyes. "You're not drunk."

Sam shook her head. Smiled again. Giggled. Twice.

"You met a boy."

Sam smiled bigger. Giggled a bit more.

Riley rolled her eyes and said, "Come on, let's go."

They walked two blocks, Samantha waiting for it . . . and then it came:

"Just don't say that I didn't warn you," Riley said, and after a long pause, "OK, tell me everything."

Sam suddenly wondered again about Riley's connection to the beautiful boy and decided if Riley did know him, she might have all sorts of stuff to say about him. Stuff that would definitely ruin this moment. So Samantha decided to keep him to herself for a little bit longer.

D DECIDES SOME THINGS ARE JUST BAD IDEAS, AND GOES HOME EARLY

It was just about midnight, but D left the bathroom — safely avoided bumping into Riley (what are the chances?) — and went straight home. He didn't even bother with a cab but decided to walk back uptown, all fifty-four blocks (although about three-quarters of the way to his destination, he started swearing at himself and hopped on the subway).

On his way home, he thought about the girl he met at the bar and he kept smiling.

He didn't have her number. He didn't even know her name, but he knew that she couldn't make a drink worth a damn and she was interesting and not like the girls he usually met, who were just trying to get drunk so they had an excuse to forget their lives each night. She was also pretty; she had this light smattering of freckles across the bridge of her nose that gave her a look of innocence — something he had never found attractive before.

He was walking up his front steps when he received a text from Riley and he cringed for a second before he read it:

Glad u stayed home 2nite?

D wondered if that was a trick question — if she saw him this evening, she was probably being sarcastic and was going to rip into him if he lied. If she hadn't seen him, and he admitted he did go out, she'd rip into him for breaking his vow already. So he played it safe and wrote:

Im always glad 2 stay home.

It was true without being true. Exactly how D liked to be. Sorta true. Until, at least, Riley wrote back:

Proud of u.

And then D felt like absolute crap. He lied to his best friend and then she had the nerve to say something as sneaky and as horrible as that she was proud of him. He was ashamed and angry — at himself, at Riley, at the random girl. Mostly at himself.

He vowed to be better (again). And behave (again). And as punishment, he wouldn't even let himself think about the random girl from the bar — in the end, getting involved with her would probably just give him one more excuse to ignore the stuff in his life he needed to do. If he was going to be good, really good, he needed to cut all that out.

And he'd start right now.

OK . . . he'd start when he woke up, because he wanted to think about how she smiled and blushed, even as she did something daring and sort of stupid behind the bar.

OK, no, he'd stop thinking about it right now.

D went upstairs, took a really cold shower, and went to bed thinking about how he'd never think about that girl ever again.

D woke up the next morning with a headache.

"I didn't even drink that much," he mumbled into his pillow. His mouth was dry, his eyes felt swollen, and like every other morning that he woke up like this (and really, it was more mornings than he'd like to remember), he knew he was going to have a raging headache all day.

He crawled out of his bed and went into the adjoining bathroom, turned on the lights, and with a groan, flipped them off again.

After his shower, he swallowed two aspirins and enough water for a small camel, and put his shades on before he even got in the elevator. He was glad he had pulled on his long heavy coat over his tailored shirt and khakis. It was cold out.

The doorman held the door open for him as he made his way outside, but he still winced at the bright light that seemed to engulf everything and make his brain pound behind his eyes.

It was going to be a long day.

He checked his watch and realized he only had a few minutes before he was supposed to meet Riley for their traditional pre-school coffee. She always got the same thing: a vanilla bean Frappuccino (which she always argued was a coffee even though the entire world knew better — but goodness help anyone who tried to convince Riley of anything) and he always got a grande iced coffee, with milk, no sugar.

He needed that coffee, so he hailed a cab and made his way to Starbucks.

Samantha met Riley outside of Starbucks about forty minutes before the first bell was supposed to ring. She had not dressed warmly enough, and stood outside shivering slightly as Riley walked up in a light jacket that fooled her by being extra puffy but not at all warm.

"Ugh, I hate winter!" Riley said. "But I love this jacket. Why does good fashion have to be so painful?"

Samantha couldn't speak without her teeth chattering, so she just shrugged.

Riley looked at her phone to check the time. "He'll probably be a little late. He always is."

Samantha had heard all about Riley's best friend, D. Back when Sam first met Riley, Samantha had learned that Riley thought she was in love with D. But then Riley had figured out that she was really in love with Eric.

If Samantha was going to be honest with herself, she was really nervous to meet Riley's oldest and best friend. What if he didn't like her — would Riley wonder if she was worth keeping as a friend?

Samantha knew she was being silly, Riley wasn't like that — she didn't care what anyone thought about her. It was just that the only time Samantha saw Riley acting un-Riley-like was in terms of D. So she wanted to make a good impression.

To mask her nervousness, she asked, "Are we going to be late for school?"

Riley rolled her eyes. "Sam, it's the first day of the spring semester, they probably won't even take attendance the first day."

"Really?"

"Everyone knows the first day is optional!"

Samantha seriously doubted that.

"Oh, brother, she's not giving the 'first day is optional' speech again, is she?" a familiar accented voice said behind her.

Riley turned and gave the guy standing behind her a huge hug, but his eyes were boring into Samantha's. And Samantha was staring back. It was THEBOY.

THEBOY was D.

D was THEBOY.

Samantha was so screwed.

#5 STAY AWAY FROM DRAMA

D looked from Riley to the girl standing next to her and then back at Riley.

"Oh, sorry," Riley said. "Samantha, this is my best friend, D. D, this is Samantha."

"Samantha," he said slowly, like he was feeling it out in his mouth. She looked like a Samantha. Last night — when he wasn't thinking about her — he tried to guess what her name was. Alexis. Amy. Corrine. Samantha was a much better fit.

"Yeah, Sam. We met last year at New Horizons. . . ." Riley let the sentence drag out. "Is everything OK in there?"

"Yeah, yeah," D said, looking at Sam, who appeared to be as confused and befuddled as he was. Apparently she wasn't expecting him to be here, of all places.

Riley turned to Sam, waved her hand in front of her face. "Hello?"

Sam blinked twice.

"Um, hi. I'm Sam." She smiled and held out her hand. "Um . . . nice to meet you?"

D grimaced a little but felt a small amount of relief that she hadn't told Riley that she had met him the night before at the bar. Sam didn't know that D wasn't supposed to be there, so she didn't know that she was saving his butt in so many words — but he was grateful anyway. He extended his hand, clasped Sam's, and said, "It's very nice to meet you."

D didn't know what to make of the face that Sam made, but she didn't look happy.

"Great, everyone is happy to meet everyone else," Riley said, already heading into Starbucks. "Can we please get some caffeine before I wilt?"

"Of course, darling," D said. Sam's eyes flew to D and he flinched, and wouldn't meet her gaze.

The two followed Riley into the coffeehouse, Riley ordering her normal sweet concoction, D ordering his normal grande, Sam ordering a tea.

"Tea?" Riley asked.

"Peppermint."

"That's not coffee, Sam," Riley said.

"I don't drink coffee."

Riley's cup stilled halfway to her lips. "But this is a Starbucks."

Sam nodded.

"You have to drink coffee in a Starbucks!"

D watched the interplay with amusement. Sam merely kept nodding and said, "You didn't order a coffee, so I figured they wouldn't kick me out either."

Riley looked at her cup. "What do you mean this isn't coffee?"

"It's not coffee, it's a Frappuccino."

"A Frappuccino is just a cold coffee."

"Um, no."

"It has the word 'uccino' in it. And the 'app' part. — Appuccino. Fra-ppuccino. It's coffee."

"Um, no."

Riley took another sip of her drink. "Well, I like it."

Sam nodded, took a sip of her tea, which was probably still hot. D laughed, and he could see Sam smile into her cup.

"I've been trying to tell her for years that it isn't coffee."

Riley squealed. "You are NOT allowed to both gang up on me."

"Aw, nobody is ganging up on you," D said, wrapping one arm around Riley's shoulders. "It's not your fault you think you drink coffee."

"If it's not coffee, what is it?"

D shrugged.

"An adult milk shake?" Sam offered helpfully. "Do you know how many calories —"

"I don't want to know!" Riley groaned. "Since I'm already depressed, let's go to class."

D kept shooting looks at Sam.

D was never what you would consider a romantic. In fact, the closest D ever got to a full-fledged romance was in the fifth grade when he sent a Valentine's Day card to Sylvia DeSalvo, who was his babysitter and a tenth grader, who laughed in his face.

D often thought about Sylvia, who was from Queens and had an accent D's father called "unintelligible," which D always thought meant something positive (well, at least until he was older), and even now he still had a warm spot in his heart for girls from Queens. But he hadn't sent a Valentine's Day card since the fifth grade and he certainly wasn't looking to start doing so again.

Love, to D, was for mothers and puppies. And sometimes only for puppies.

But that didn't stop him from having all his attention zeroed in on Samantha.

What a mess.

#6 MAKE NEW FRIENDS

Aside from Riley, Sam hadn't made a new friend since she was fourteen. Which didn't exactly help her stress level when walking into the Curtis Prep lunchroom. Excuse me, cafeteria.

Located in the middle of the school, the cafeteria was larger than her last school's library. It was a big square room, and all around the edges were small stations where students could pick up items or full lunches to bring back to the little café tables that took up all the room in between.

Sam was going to have a panic attack.

Riley wasn't in the same lunch period as she was, and Sam hadn't really thought to try to meet people during her classes. It was as if everyone else had their friends already; their groups and cliques were already set. And now they all sat together in their little groups. There was a table of cheerleaders and what she imagined were lacrosse players, since half of them were waving their lacrosse sticks in the air above their heads while a teacher tried to get them to stop. There was a group of quiet students bent over books, who looked like they sat together so they wouldn't have to sit with anyone else. Everyone else seemed like a more general mix, but walking through the group toward the lunch line, she heard their conversations . . . and realized that there were definitely cliques at Curtis Prep.

Samantha got on the lunch line (she had no idea that some school cafeterias were called cafés and served fresh pizza and sushi). She got a bowl of edamame (which are soybeans, for those of you who don't know) and a slice of vegetarian delight pizza (which is pizza with vegetables, for those of you who don't know), and then went into the café to find somewhere to sit.

She was starting to freak out, looking at the sea of faces (none of which she recognized), and couldn't even find a seat that looked promising — or any empty table — and as her mind catalogued all the places where she might be able to eat alone (the girls' bathroom? the library? outside?), someone tapped her on her shoulder, making her jump, and her edamame went everywhere (the pizza stayed put).

"I'm sorry, I didn't mean to startle you," D said, trying to steady her tray with one hand. Samantha readjusted the tray in her arms, balancing a 1% milk along with an apple that she would snack on later. Even if the apple had just rolled onto her pizza and was now hot and a little cheesy.

"You didn't. I mean, you did, but I don't mind." Sam scrunched up her nose a little. She had NO idea what she was saying and was talking like an absolute idiot. But this was the boy that Riley had been in love with just about a year ago. This was the boy who asked for her number just about twenty-four hours ago.

"Uh, OK," D said. "I just wanted to know if you'd like to sit with us."

"Um, no, I'm fine. Really, it's OK. Actually, yes," she mumbled quickly.

D stared at her for a moment.

"Shall I follow you?" Sam asked.

"Yeah, yeah," he said, turning and walking to a far corner, where the round tables were huddled in a small group. He motioned toward a table and jerked his head to the others so they would move over and make a place for Sam.

"Hi," Sam said, placing her tray down on the table. It took up most of the space and Sam realized no one else had a tray. In fact, most of them (well, the female ones) didn't even have any food in front of them.

One of the girls looked at Samantha's tray and muttered, "I think I'm going to be ill." And she got up and walked away in her size-zero pants.

D turned to watch her go with a strange expression on her face.

"I know," Sam said. "So much food, so little time." She smiled, plunked down in her chair, and while the others looked on, shoved a huge bite of pizza into her mouth. "*Mmmmmm*, this is SO good."

She wiped her mouth and drank a big gulp of milk. She realized she was going overboard, but didn't these girls know that one slice of pizza never killed anyone? It was certainly better than not eating at all.

"Aren't you worried about the calories?" asked one of the girls, with a pointed look at Sam's midsection.

"Sure." She took another huge bite and D smirked. One of the other boys laughed outright.

As Sam chewed she could feel her mind rebelling. Calories! Carbs! Processed food! Sam slowly made resolutions with herself that she'd go to the gym and do extra cardio to make up for it. But the occasional pizza wasn't going to kill her, and it was worth shoving it into her mouth to make the non-eaters gawk.

Maybe extra gym time today *and* tomorrow.

You could take the girl out of New Horizons, but perhaps you couldn't yank the New Horizons out of the girl.

"I'm Justin." The boy who had laughed was looking at Sam and holding out his hand.

Samantha wiped her hands together to remove the crumbs and shook his hand. "Samantha."

"Samantha is a good friend of Riley's," D said by way of introduction.

"Oh, *you* are Riley's friend," said the calorie girl.

"Yes, and you are?"

"I'm Marley."

"It's nice to meet you, Marley," Sam said, chomping down another bite.

Marley smiled politely and then turned her head away to talk to a friend about something that included shopping, vacations, and what was on television that night.

"So, Sam — you're new?" Justin asked.

Samantha took a good look at Justin and realized exactly what he was. If eighties teen movies had taught Samantha anything, it was the fact that in every school there was one boy who seemed to walk the line between different groups — which means that he can flirt and date anyone he wants: a jock girl, a preppy girl, a popular girl, and nobody would blink if he went out with the dorkiest girl in school — because, if she were dating him, she would be above reproach. He had an easy manner about him, Sam could tell from the way he sat. He felt like all he had to do was shower his affection on a girl and she would fall madly in love with him. It was probably true.

He had beautiful, blond boy-next-door looks but something in his eyes screamed "troublemaker." And the dimple that appeared in his half smile didn't help.

Samantha looked at D, who was shooting Justin a pretty evil stink eye.

"Yeah, my first day."

"Wow, switching school your senior year — that must be tough."

Samantha thought about it for a moment. "It's harder than I thought it would be, but I'm still glad I did it."

"So am I," Justin said, smiling at her, until D coughed and Justin leaned back in his chair and Samantha blushed again, looking at D.

"Can I walk you to your next class, Samantha?" D asked, with a pointed look at Justin, who just raised his eyebrows in response.

"Yeah, I mean — yes, that would be lovely," Sam said, gathering her things while she stuck her apple in her bag, not failing to notice a little smirk that D shot Justin's way.

"I'll be right back. I'm going to go grab a drink," D said. "Want something?"

Sam shook her head.

Samantha watched D walk away and she might ("might," I'm not saying she did) have checked him out just a little.

"Tell me you aren't interested in him," Justin said, sidling into the chair next to Samantha's that D had recently vacated.

"Who?"

Justin nodded in the direction that D had walked away, and Sam lowered her glance when D turned around to catch her staring. "I'm not, I mean, I don't really know him."

"Then it's much easier to be interested," Justin said, smiling at her.

Perhaps it was because Samantha was too busy watching

D walk away (and it was an amazing sight), or perhaps because she wasn't used to interacting with that many guys — having attended an all-girls boarding school for so long — or maybe it was just because she didn't think anyone could possibly fall in love with her after five seconds of watching her shove a pizza slice into her mouth but, Samantha knew — almost instinctively — not to take anything Justin said or did too seriously.

"Yes, I suppose it is."

"Do you think it would be just as easy to be interested in me?" he asked. He held her gaze and Samantha wanted to break it but felt like that would be losing some little game that she didn't know the rules of.

"I think," she replied, "that there would be absolutely nothing *easy* about being interested in you."

Justin nodded slightly, and then laughed. The sharp look in his eyes, the one where he was assessing and pulling strings, went away. And Samantha felt herself relax as a real smile, a warm one, replaced the one he had previously been giving her. "Samantha, I think we might become very good friends."

Samantha smiled. "I think I might like that."

"That is," Justin said, raising his voice slightly, "unless you think we could be more than just friends?"

Sam looked at him askew for a second before realizing that D had come to stand right behind her.

"I'm not sure," D cut in, holding a soda in one hand, "that you two should be friends."

"Aw," Justin said, standing up and patting D roughly on the back, "don't be jealous, Hammond." He winked at Samantha and then walked away, leaving D scowling behind him. Samantha laughed at the easy way Justin played D right then. It was almost as if D *was* jealous. But that was silly. . . .

When Justin was out of earshot, D turned to Samantha. "I know he's good-looking and very charming, but that kid is a complete scoundrel."

"Are you warning me away?"

"No," D said, flummoxed. "I mean, it's up to you. I just . . ."

Sam put her hand on D's arm. "I understand."

D's chest rose and lowered with a deep breath.

"So, do you know where B-thirty-three is?" Samantha asked, taking her hand away and pulling out her schedule.

"Yes."

Samantha stood, looked around, and waited. D stood and waited too.

"Would you mind telling me where it is?"

"Oh, uh, yeah . . . I can show you."

Sam smiled to herself, tipping her head so her short hair drifted to cover her face. Sam loved walking down the halls with him. She didn't like the dirty looks the girls of Curtis Prep shot her way, but when D motioned for her to turn by placing his hand on her lower back . . . she felt it was worth it. He was worth it. She wanted to kiss him. The minute the thought entered her head she felt warm all over (in all the usual and some new surprising places). She thought about how shocked he'd be if she just pushed him up against the nearby lockers or the wrestling team's trophy cabinet and kissed him.

"Here it is," he said, pausing by the door.

She laughed nervously and practically dove through the door — embarassed by her thoughts — without even saying good-bye.

D TRIES TO FIGURE OUT WHICH FRIENDS HE COULD LOSE

D was standing with Riley outside the front steps of the school. D was pretending to be reading the community notice board posted outside of the brick-face building, while Riley tried to avoid a large woman walking down the sidewalk with three small dogs.

"So what was up with you and Samantha this morning?"

"I don't know what you mean," D said. He leaned against the wall and looked down the street as a group of students filed out the front doors. He scanned the group for Samantha. Again.

"She's staying after to work on her writing sample," Riley said.

"I *really* don't know what you mean."

"Right," she said.

"Fine. What do you think is going on?"

Riley watched him carefully. "I have no idea or I wouldn't be asking. But if she liked you —"

"You think she likes me?" he said before he had a chance to gauge the excitement in his voice.

Riley watched D, while he did his best to shrug in his most careless, uncaring way possible.

"I mean . . . " He faltered. He didn't know what to say.

"She's worked really hard to get into college, you know," Riley said. "She needs to write a new sample, but she has it in her head that she needs to go to this one program or she won't be happy."

"I understand that. I feel like I need NOT to go to this one program or I won't be happy."

"You know, she has her own list. . . ." Riley said softly.

"Really?"

Riley nodded. "Well, just be careful, OK?"

"What's that supposed to mean?" D asked, turning to face his best friend.

"She's just not used to . . . people like you."

"That's great, Riley. Exactly what kind of person am I?"

Riley stepped closer to D, put her arm around his waist and her head on his shoulder. "You're amazing, D. You're an amazing friend and a good guy — but you're not exactly the poster child for good boyfriend behavior."

D wanted to protest — he felt vaguely annoyed that his best friend thought of him as such a "bad" person. But he figured that she probably had a point, so he kept his mouth shut and instead felt slightly depressed.

Before D could respond she continued, "And maybe you need to figure your stuff out, you know? Because what happens if Samantha's list conflicts with your own?"

D blew out a deep breath and rocked his head back. Riley rubbed his back gently.

"You know I love you, right?" she asked.

"Yeah, I know."

"I want you to be happy. I don't think that you'd be happy knowing you hurt her for no reason."

"No."

"That's all I'm saying," Riley said. "I'm going home. Do you want to come?"

"No, I'm going . . ." His voice trailed off as he looked down the street. He had nowhere to be and nowhere to go.

"Call me later," Riley said, waving.

"Yeah, bye, sweetheart," he said, while she walked off in the opposite direction, leaving him alone with his thoughts. Samantha had a list too? What was she trying to change about her life?

Maybe her life was really horrible, or she really *was* like everyone else. Perhaps, D thought, if he got to know her, he would realize that she wasn't that special. Yes, that was definitely the way to go.

. . . And D went searching for Samantha.

*   *   *

Twenty minutes later, D wished he had asked Riley where Samantha was hiding out because he felt like he had combed the entire school. He had started in the library's computer lab, then went through the east and west wings, he checked the café, and even called her name into the girls' bathrooms on both levels of the building. The only thing he knew for sure was that Curtis Prep was too big. And he was pretty sure that Samantha was invisible. At least to him.

When he was about to give up, he decided to take another stroll through the library before going home, and that's where he found her, in the rear of the stacks, bent over a MacBook and punching the keys.

"I do boxing, but I guess that looks like a good way of working off some extra aggression," he said, leaning over her.

"Oh, hey," she said, looking somewhat startled to see him. She leaned the screen down so he couldn't see what she was writing, and after a second, relaxed and smiled at him.

"Busy?"

"Um, a little . . . I'm . . ."

"Writing, Riley told me."

Samantha smiled and shrugged. "Trying to write, but right now I'd be having as much luck as if this *were* a punching bag."

"Not flowing, eh?"

"Not at all," she said, leaning back in her chair. "What are you doing here?"

Good question, D thought. "I'm . . . I'm just trying to get a little studying done."

Samantha tilted her head and looked at him in a way that made him want to squirm. "I didn't take you for the studying-in-the-library-after-school type."

"You got me. I was looking for you."

"I'd like to say that you are inhibiting my artistic process, but really, I'm like a dry well right now. So pull up a chair. Maybe you'll inspire me," she said, gesturing to a chair that was nearby.

D pulled the chair over. He looked at the pile of papers that were strewn around Samantha's cubby. "So you take this writing stuff really seriously, huh?"

"It's what I've always wanted to do."

D nodded.

"How about you?" she asked. "What do you do?"

"Oh, you know, I drink, I party, I woo women," D said with a smirk.

"I've heard." Samantha looked disappointed by his answer, and D settled uneasily into the chair.

"I guess I don't really do anything."

"Everyone does something," she said. "What do you want to do?"

"I don't know," D said, shifting his feet. "I don't really *do* much of anything. I hang out, I suppose."

Samantha sat quietly, observing him. He felt the need to fill the silence so he just kept talking. "When I'm alone, I like to play."

"Play?"

"You know, like the piano."

"Really?" she said. "I didn't take you for the piano-playing type either."

"Yes, well, that and studying in the library," he said, with a self-deprecating laugh. This was not going as well as he had hoped, but then again, with Sam he never really knew what it was he was hoping for. So perhaps it was going well. "Actually, my mother taught me to play. She was a pianist, a pretty good one."

"She doesn't play anymore?"

"She died a few years ago," D said.

"Oh," Samantha said quietly, tucking her hair behind her ears. "I'm sorry, I didn't know."

"No, it's fine," D said, wishing he had kept his big mouth shut. "It's . . . Yeah. It's whatever."

"So, you play."

"Not as much anymore, but I used to play all the time," D said, thankful that she didn't dwell on it. "That's how Riley and I met. We took piano lessons with the same instructor. Her classes were before mine and we'd bump into each other all the time. We figured out that we were both motherless and, I dunno, I think she just tried to adopt me or something."

"Riley plays the piano?" Samantha asked. "I mean, the rest sounds like Riley, but *piano*?"

"She definitely plays. Poorly. Very, very poorly. I think she might have figured out 'Chopsticks' before she turned to a more natural hobby."

Samantha just shot him a questioning look, so D filled in the answer with: "Shopping."

"Ah," Samantha said, nodding. "Everyone is good at something."

"And Riley is a pro at shopping."

There was a weird silence for a couple of seconds, before D stood up and said, "Well, I have to get going."

"Oh, um, of course," Samantha said, nodding.

"I'll let you get back to your writing." He picked up his bag, flinging the strap over his shoulder and straightening it over his coat. "See you." He turned to leave.

"I'd like to hear you play sometime," Sam said.

D turned around to face her. "I'd like to read your writing sometime."

Sam smiled. "It's a date." When D smiled, she stuttered, "I mean, not a *date*-date, but like, we can do that. If you want. I mean . . ."

"I want," D said softly.

"Yeah, me too," Sam said, calm again.

"Well . . ."

"Absolutely!" Sam said. "Back to the grind!" she said, before twisting her face into a somewhat confused look. D laughed and walked away, hearing Sam mutter behind him, "Back to the grind?"

She was cute, D decided. Too cute.

#7 ASK A BOY OUT

D wasn't at Starbucks the next morning, and when he wasn't at lunch either, Sam started to wonder if he was avoiding her. After their chat the afternoon before, Sam had thought there was more to D than other people realized. There was definitely more to him than Sam had realized, and she wanted to know more.

Sam had decided that she was going to do number seven on her list: ask a boy out. She spent most of the night awake in bed, restless, thinking of ways that she could do it. Maybe in the morning over coffee she could ask if he had seen the new James Bond movie. What if he said no? Worse, what if he said yes? Samantha needed some sort of plan.

Maybe if she just showed him she was interested, he'd take the hint and ask her out. He had asked for her number, after all, and that was when he didn't even know her. Could it be that now that he had gotten to know her a little, he didn't want to ask her out?

"What are you thinking about? You look so serious," Justin said. She still sat at D's table, even though he wasn't there. And while the rest of the table pretty much ignored her, Justin spent the entire lunch period trying to flirt with her while the girls rolled their eyes.

"Nobody. I mean, nothing."

"Not very convincing, Samantha Owens," Justin said, a smile playing around the corner of his mouth. He was very good-looking. Samantha thought, *Why don't I feel even half of what I feel for D when I look at Justin?* He seemed way more interested in her than D did. . . .

"What are you doing this weekend?"

"Writing, probably," Sam answered.

"Oh, a writer?" Justin asked.

"A wannabe writer," Sam corrected him.

"Well, how about you let me take you out and we'll find a good story for you to write?"

Sam smiled politely and said, "I think that's a bad idea, Justin. Wouldn't that ruin our friendship?"

He laughed and said, "OK, but I only take no the first time around. Next time I ask, I expect a completely different answer." Then he dropped an apple on her bag and walked away.

It wasn't exactly romantic, but it was really sweet.

Later that afternoon, Riley went home with Samantha so they could watch reruns of *Top Chef* in Samantha's den. Her father had cleared out, mumbling something under his breath but moving copies of books and other newspapers out of the way so the girls could splay themselves out on Samantha's mother's blue-checkered, oversized couches with cups of tea and low-fat cookies.

"So, Justin asked me out today," Samantha said.

"Justin asked you out?"

"Yeah, I mean, I think so. He asked me if I wanted to do —"

"Yeah, yeah, he asked you out. I don't distrust your interpretation of the events, I'm just surprised."

Samantha blushed furiously, embarrassed that Riley didn't think someone as good-looking as Justin could be interested in her.

"Yeah, I was a little surprised too," she said.

Riley looked confused and glanced at Samantha. "Why were you surprised?"

"I mean, he's . . . y'know . . ."

"An absolute player who hasn't ever asked anyone out in the history of my having known him?"

"What?" Samantha asked.

"Yeah, that's why I'm surprised. I've never heard of him asking anyone out before."

"Oh," Samantha said, and then she turned red for a different reason.

"So, are you going to go out with him?"

"I don't think so."

Then Riley gave her another sharp look before grabbing the remote and muting the television.

"Hey, that was *Top Chef*! I wanted to watch that."

"Justin asks you out and you said . . ."

"I said that I thought it was a bad idea."

"Were you playing hard to get?"

"No, I think I was saying that I thought it was a *bad idea*."

"But you weren't just saying that to play hard to get?"

"No," she said, trying to grab the remote back from Riley, but Riley had fast reflexes and quickly moved it away from Sam's reach.

"You said no."

"Yes."

"I think you are crazy."

"Riley, I noticed. What's your point?"

"My point is that there is absolutely no reason to say no, I mean aside from the fact that he's an outrageous flirt, but it would be fun! Just don't sleep with him."

"Riley!"

"Fine, sleep with him if you want. . . ."

"I don't want!"

"Then why are you yelling?" Riley asked casually.

Samantha took a deep breath. "I'm not yelling. I'm simply saying that I'm not going to date Justin."

"Who are you going to date, then?"

"What do you mean?" Samantha said.

"Don't play dumb with me!"

"Who's playing?"

"Sam, if you're waiting around for D to —"

"I'm not waiting around for anything," Sam said, grabbing the remote and turning the volume back up on the television.

"Do you like him?"

Sam took a really deep breath. "Is that weird?"

"Why would it be weird?"

"Because of your history with him," Sam said. She turned the television off and looked around to see if anyone would overhear their conversation. Riley was looking at her with a very serious expression. At least serious for Riley.

"Our history is just that, history," Riley said. "I think that if you two have a chance at finding something like I found with Eric, you need to pursue it."

"Really? You're not just saying that?"

"Really." The two girls smiled shyly at each other. "You should ask him to the Spring Fling; it's in a few weeks."

Samantha turned a little pink. "Should I just wait for him to ask me?"

"Waiting for a guy to do the asking is like waiting for world peace; sounds like a great idea — but who knows when it'll actually happen." Sam laughed and tossed a pillow at her friend, who grabbed it and tucked it under her arm. "I think you should ask him, Sam."

Sam didn't want to ask him. She wanted to be asked, but she figured she could be the brave one. She could pick up the phone and dial him and just see if he already had a date to the dance. It wouldn't be that difficult.

But that was an hour ago, and she was still sitting on her bed staring at his number in her cell phone. And she hadn't called yet.

There was a knock on the door. "Come in!" Samantha called, tucking her cell phone under the pillow of her bed.

"Hey, Sam?" Andrew said, peeking his head into her room.

"Hi, Andy . . . I mean, Andrew. Come in," she said, sitting up on her bed.

"Uh, hey. So I have a question."

"Shoot."

He looked really nervous standing there, shuffling his feet.

"Is everything OK, Andrew?"

"Yeah, everything is fine. It's about a girl."

Samantha had a major "aw" moment. Her little brother had a girlfriend. She giggled, and Andrew's eyes grew wide and he turned red. Apparently blushing was a family trait.

"I'm sorry, it's just . . . you're such an adult, y'know?"

"Yeah, well, not that much of an adult, I guess."

Samantha patted her bedspread and Andrew came over and perched awkwardly on the edge of her bed. After readjusting several times, he finally settled in.

"There is this girl at school. She's an artist."

"Wow."

"And a poet."

"Ah."

Andrew grimaced. "Anyway, I wanted to ask her out but wasn't sure how to do it."

"Oh, Andrew, I'm not sure I'm going to be of any help."

"You're a girl. How would you want a guy to ask you out?"

Samantha thought for a moment and then answered as honestly as possible. "I'd want it to be as simple and as straightforward as possible. I think I'd like the guy to say, 'Hi. I really like you, I think you're smart and funny and pretty, and I'd like to spend time with you.'"

Samantha was really proud of herself; that sounded like good advice.

"That sounds . . . lame."

Samantha choked. "Um, I guess. But it's what I want to hear. And I think that if someone is interested in me and they were able to be that brave to say so . . . I'd respect that."

"Oh."

Samantha smiled.

"Still lame," he said.

"Fine, then I have a question for you."

"So . . . there is this guy . . ." And Samantha told him about her plan to ask D to the dance. "So, should I call him?"

"He should call you."

Samantha frowned. "He doesn't have my number."

"If he was interested, he could get it."

"You give crappy advice."

Andrew laughed. "Call if you want, but . . ."

"Thanks so much."

Andrew got up and walked toward the door. "I think guys are way easier to figure out. If we like someone, we pursue them, if we don't — we don't."

"And you know this about all men because . . ."

"Because I am one?"

"Right, get out."

"Are you going to —"

"None of your business!" Sam cried, hurling a pillow at Andrew while he was halfway through the door.

"Touchy . . ."

But he singsonged a "good luck" before shutting the door behind him.

Samantha pulled the phone out from under her other pillow and propped the pillow against the headboard of her bed.

She scrolled through the contacts until she found THEBOY and, after a couple of moments of hesitation, hit the CALL button.

It rang twice before someone picked up the phone and, in a very annoyed voice, snapped, "Hello."

"Um, hi, may I speak with . . . um, Michael?"

A heavy sigh was on the other end of the receiver, "This is he, who is this?"

"Um, hi."

"Hello?"

"Um, yes, hi, it's Samantha. Riley's friend?" Samantha wanted to just hang up — this wasn't going at all the way she had hoped it would go.

"Oh, hey. Sorry about the way I answered, I was expecting someone else."

"Oh." Another girl? Was he expecting another girl to call? Samantha felt like a complete idiot. "Well, I don't want to keep you if you are expecting a call — we can talk tomorrow at school." More like Sam could now avoid D as much as he was avoiding her, so he would never see how embarrassed she was to have made such an idiot out of herself.

"No, no," he said quickly. "Please. So . . . what do you want to talk about?"

Samantha belatedly realized that having made the effort to actually call a boy, she didn't exactly have a plan beyond what would happen if he picked up the phone.

She babbled for a few minutes about nothing. About the weather (wasn't it so cold!) and about school (wasn't it so boring!) and about life and parents (weren't they such a chore!). And then out of nowhere, Sam blurted, "Have you been avoiding me?"

She heard a really deep sigh and silence.

"You have, and then I called you. Wow, this is awkward," Sam said.

"No, it's not," he replied.

"Oh no, it's definitely awkward."

"I don't want this to be awkward."

"Too late. It's awkward. Awkwardness abounds. I'm immersed in awkwardness."

"Wow, that's a lot of awkward," D said.

"Absolutely."

"Anything I can do?"

"A swift kick to the head would probably work."

"How about this: Hang up the phone."

"What?" Sam asked.

"Just hang up the phone."

"Um, OK . . . bye?"

"Bye." And the line disconnected. Sam stared at it for a moment before getting a little upset, but before she could really react (and this was a good thing), the phone started buzzing in her hand. The display said THEBOY, and Sam smiled and hit the CALL button again.

"Hello?" she answered.

"Now I called you," D said on the other side of the line. "No longer awkward."

Sam laughed and snuggled into her pillows, the phone tucked under her left ear, while she concentrated on the cuticles of her right hand. "Actually, I was going to call you," she said.

"Oh? What a coincidence."

"Yes, I was going to see if you wanted to do something this weekend."

"Um . . . well, I actually . . ." D stuttered. "I have plans, but . . ."

"No, no, it's fine!" Sam said, burying her face into her pillow. The phone smushed against her shoulder, so she could only grasp fragments of what D was saying. But none of it sounded too good.

". . . but want to . . . after school . . . free . . ."

"No, no, it's fine!" Sam repeated, feeling extra stupid. Of course she should have waited for him to ask her. Since he hadn't, he obviously didn't want to go out with her. How could she have been so dumb? "Actually, I have to go."

"Sam . . ."

"Really, I have to go."

"OK, if you *really* have to go."

Samantha's eyes stung. "Yeah, I really have to go."

"Bye, Samantha."

"Bye, D."

Samantha hung up the phone and threw it to the other edge of the bed and then buried her face into the pillow. Tears filled her eyes. She had never been so humiliated in her life and she had never wanted to disappear quite like she did just then. She sniffed, her nose running.

Well, Samantha tried to tell herself, that was the first time she ever asked a boy out and the first time she was ever turned down. She supposed it had to have happened sometime. Maybe it was better to have it happen now, with D. Because now she wouldn't be waiting around for him to call, and wouldn't be looking for him at school. In fact, she was happy he said no. He was way too . . . something.

It was going to be humiliating at school tomorrow.

Andrew stuck his head back in the room. "How did it go?"

"Ugh!" Samantha said, throwing herself back on her pillows.

"Is the wound too fresh to say I told you so?"

Sam threw her other pillow at her brother. He laughed, closing the door once again.

Sam picked up the phone and texted Riley:

He said no.

Riley texted back:

That idiot.

82

And her phone started ringing a second later. "I'll kill him!" Riley yelled when Sam answered.

"No, no, it's fine!" Sam said, wondering when she started to sound like a broken record.

"It's absolutely *not* fine. If I didn't know that he felt —"

"Riley, I just want to forget this night ever happened," Samantha said. "I'm completely embarrassed and I don't know how I'll face him tomorrow at school."

"You have nothing to be embarrassed about! And if that turd doesn't want to be your date to the dance, we'll just find you another date. Someone more worthy of your attention."

"Yeah, I thought of that," Sam said. "I need help. . . ."

"I am *so* there. We'll figure it out tomorrow. Just try and get some sleep and wear something extra cute tomorrow, OK?"

Sam sniffed and swallowed hard. When she got off the phone she took a deep breath and threw it on the floor, and tried her best to get some sleep, like Riley suggested.

D CHANGES HIS MIND AND TRIES TO ASK SAMANTHA OUT

The next morning D left home early. He had barely slept the night before, tossing and turning and trying to figure out why he hadn't just told Sam that he had sworn he'd stay home all weekend working on his applications. It made him sound like he didn't want to go out with her, when he really *did* want to go out with her. But this was an easy enough fix, D figured. He'd just get to Starbucks early, before even Riley got there, and he'd ask Sam out. For real.

But he was too early and was nervous to boot, so he took a walk around the block (like four times), so that he wouldn't look like he had been standing on the sidewalk freezing his ass off (for thirty minutes).

How would he explain all this to her? D didn't know. He'd just figure it out when she showed up . . . if she showed up. And if he was really lucky, she'd be so happy that they were actually going out, he wouldn't have to explain his foul-up on the phone.

But unfortunately for D, Samantha showed up right on time, with Riley Swain.

"Damn," D muttered under his breath, watching the two walking up the street together, their heads bowed near each other's like they were sharing some sort of secret. Riley was talking and Sam was shaking her head. D smiled at the pair; they looked like friends *should* look.

And then D's stomach clenched. Maybe they were talking about him — maybe Riley was warning her away from him — would she do that? Probably not. Maybe Sam was telling Riley what an ass D had been on the phone last night and then Riley would tell Sam about all the girls D had fooled around with in the past, all the girls he had blown off, and Sam would blow him off too.

Because, and D could tell, Sam was a "good girl." Riley had been absolutely right about that, Sam wasn't the kind of girl you should toy with. You were either serious about her or you weren't; if you were — well, great, but if you weren't and you respected her, you should stay away.

When he decided to ask her out . . . he had been thinking (the night before, while he tried not to think about her — again) about the things that she might like to do. He'd like to show her the city, maybe bring her to a museum, maybe out to dinner or a Broadway show. He thought she'd like that. Or maybe to a comedy club to see some bad jokes being told. She'd laugh, and D had smiled at the image.

But standing there on the sidewalk watching his best friend and the girl he was starting to think of as *his friend* walking up the street, he was a mixture of nervous and anxious — unable to quite pinpoint why he felt the way he did.

And it was too late to take a walk around the block once more, so he stuck his hands in his jeans pockets and waited. Both girls, coming upon him, looked a little shocked to see him.

He gave Riley a kiss on the cheek, as was their custom, and then — awkwardly looked at Sam. He leaned over to give her a friendly kiss too. She put out her hand to shake, jabbing her fingers into his sternum. They both jerked back, and then to cover it up, both jerked back together again, him with his hand up, her going to kiss him on the cheek, and he was pretty sure he brushed against her breast that time.

She flared red, and D took her by the shoulders and pulled her closer, fast, and when she went to kiss him on the cheek and he went to kiss her, he ended up kissing the corner of her mouth instead.

They both stood back.

"Well, that was interesting," Riley said. "Want another go? I can take a walk. . . ."

"Shut up, Riley," Sam said.

"Yes, please do," D said.

Riley just laughed. "I'm going to go get my non-coffee. You two?"

"Yes, I'm going to get my non-coffee too," Sam said, walking in behind her.

D watched the girls walk into the shop, and then groaned loudly and rubbed his hands down his face. This was going to be impossible.

They walked slowly toward school with their drinks in hand. D took small sips of his coffee and listened in on their conversation — which neither made an attempt to include him in on.

D was a little peeved — he had been Riley's morning "coffee date" for the past four years and now he was being excluded unceremoniously. He tried to tune the girls out and pretend he had better things to think about than whatever they were discussing, but when the word "date" came up and burned into his conscious brain, D started paying attention.

"Well, the Spring Fling is held every March, and that's coming up really fast. If we are going to find you the right date for that . . ." Riley was saying. Samantha was nodding.

". . . so . . ." Riley continued, "I think that we can whittle down the list to just a couple —"

"A couple?" D cut in.

"Like three or four," Riley said over her shoulder.

D was obviously eavesdropping by this point, and feeling slightly guilty about it, despite the fact that they shouldn't have

87

been talking about this in front of him if they didn't want him to hear. Or maybe they did want him to hear?

"I was thinking of Trey Parker," Riley said.

Riley shot D a look and he deadpanned his face, raising his hands in the air as if to say he was innocent.

"And Martin Ford."

D snorted.

"I also think you'd like Jordan Laermer," Riley said, before flashing D a death stare because he started laughing.

"What is this for?" D asked.

"I told Samantha I'd help her find a date to the Spring Fling," Riley said calmly, daring D to laugh.

"And these are the guys you want to send her with?" D said, almost shouting.

"What's wrong with them?" Riley shouted back.

"Are you trying to turn the poor girl off men entirely?" D asked once he could catch his breath. Samantha's eyes volleyed between the two friends. "I mean, Jordan Laermer?"

"Jordan is a very nice boy," Riley said, making a face.

"Jordan still carries around his retainer."

"So?"

"He stopped using it in the eighth grade," D said pointedly.

"Oh, gross," Riley said. She turned to Samantha. "I didn't know *that*."

"Of course not," D said, puffing up his chest. "There are some things you just won't know."

"That's all right, Riley," Samantha said. "I think anyone you choose will be fine."

"Thanks, Sam."

D looked at both of them incredulously. "How about me?" he spit out before he had a chance to really think. Both girls looked at him as if he had grown a second head. And he coughed a little. "I mean, first of all, Riley's taste in men is somewhat suspect." (Riley coughed and sputtered.) "Two, the guys from Curtis Prep are somewhat suspect and there are things about them that you girls would never, ever know."

"What do you suggest?" Riley asked, arching her eyebrows.

They had arrived at the school and D stood on the step, watching the crowd of students swarm in. He nodded to a couple that said hi to him and to the girls, and then said, "Well, why don't you just run any potential candidates by me?"

At this, Samantha shot him a death glare of the first order. If her eyes had been attached to any type of laser beams, D would be in a death glare puddle right now.

But Riley was looking at D, assessing, before saying, "You think this would be better by committee?"

"Two heads are better than one, Riley darling."

If Samantha was going to be going on dates, and there was nothing D could do to stop her, at the very least he could make sure he knew who she was going out with and maybe . . . control the damage. The idea of her going out with someone who she actually could and would like made him feel slightly sick, and if he had more experience with the emotion, D would have realized that he was jealous.

"Dating by committee?" Riley asked.

Sam started to shake her head at the same time Riley broke into a smile and cried, "Brilliant!"

And D wondered what he had gotten himself into.

SAMANTHA LETS OTHERS FIND HER A DATE (SINCE SHE OBVIOUSLY CAN'T GET HER OWN) (GOOD WORK, D)

Marley & Brendan are meeting us in the library after school, 3:45. x Riley

Samantha walked into the library holding her notebook and calculus book across her chest like armor. She had never felt so intimidated entering a library before, and she wasn't sure she liked the change.

She walked past the row of students sitting in the reading room and past the AV equipment until she hit the stacks, and in the back there were five chairs pulled into a smooshed little circle. There sat Riley, sitting primly on a chair, wearing small reading glasses that Sam knew weren't hers (especially since they didn't have any lenses), while leaning over her iPhone.

Sam recognized Marley from lunch and another boy, who Sam assumed was Brendan. They were all pointing at whatever Riley had on her iPhone and were arguing animatedly about whatever was written there. D was standing in the back, leaning against one of the tall shelves of books, pursing his lips in a very not-amused manner.

Sam was just nervous.

"Hi, everyone," she said, when she realized none of them would notice her entrance.

Riley looked up and gave her a big smile, D nodded in her direction, Marley gave her a glance, but Brendan jumped up and gave her a big hug. She liked him right away, even though his short, spiky hair poked her annoyingly in the nose when he hugged her. He was short, even though his dark hair was gelled so high that it gave him an additional inch or two.

"OK, can we get this over with?" Marley asked. "Some of us have lives to get back to."

"Really? Like who?" Riley asked.

Marley just pointed at the paper.

"So, we were just coming up with a couple of names as possible Spring Fling dates," Riley said, moving things around on her touch screen.

Sam looked at each of the group's members. Brendan was nodding vigorously, very excited (obviously) to be there. D looked like he wanted to die. Marley looked like she wanted everyone else to die.

D looked up and Sam looked away quickly. She wondered what he thought about all this. Was he jealous? Sam realized she wanted him to be, which was silly — he had no reason to be jealous . . . he didn't even like her.

D plucked Riley's iPhone from her hands and glanced at the list.

"You can't be serious!" D yelled. A librarian walking by shushed him loudly and D repeated it again, softer this time. "Samantha, this is insane, you can't really be so desperate as to want to date any one of these idiots."

The word "desperate" was a bad one to use; Samantha flinched at it, as did the rest of the group.

"It's not about being desperate," Riley assured her. "It's about being open to new possibilities."

Sam thought about it — wasn't that what her time here was all about? Trying new things? She slowly nodded. "I want to do it."

"Ugh," D said, dropping into his seat.

"You don't have to be here if this is against your moral code or something," Riley told him.

"Don't think you're doing this without me," D said. "Someone has to protect this girl's best interests. And you three are obviously off your rockers."

"D," Sam started to cut in to defend her friends. Well, at least defend Riley.

"I'm not even going to start on you," D said, pointing a finger at Samantha.

"I don't know," Brendan said. "I think it sounds like fun. Maybe I should do it myself."

"One at a time," Riley said, plucking her phone back from D's grasp. "OK, back to the list!"

Sam left the library with a small sense of foreboding and a huge, huge headache. They now had a list and a plan. She said good-bye to the group outside the library and walked in the direction of her parents' apartment, and after a few steps, realized she was being followed by D.

She turned to face him. "Are you following me?"

"Um, my apartment is in this direction."

"Oh."

D nodded. "It wouldn't seem like I was following you if you allowed me to escort you home."

Sam nodded and D caught up with her and then fell in line, walking together up the sidewalk, sometimes bumping into each other when a larger group would walk by in the opposite direction.

At Lexington and 50th they had to avoid a bunch of women and men in suits leaving dry cleaners and small food shops as they hurried from work to home; there were nannies pushing strollers and people walking dogs. Sam and D had to walk very closely next to each other to avoid them all.

Once in a while their arms would bump while they walked, and Sam would feel a sizzle of energy jump up her arm. She willed herself to believe that D was just like anyone else. She willed herself to make small talk so he wouldn't know how much he was affecting her.

But they didn't talk. They walked six blocks before either spoke a word to the other, until Sam couldn't take the silence anymore and said, "I'm sorry about putting you on the spot the other night."

"There is absolutely nothing to apologize for," D said softly.

"I feel like I put you in an uncomfortable position, and —"

"Not at all."

"But you're friends with my friend, and now I feel kind of awkward," she explained as she readjusted her backpack on her shoulders.

"Don't feel awkward, there is absolutely nothing to feel awkward about." Sam figured he meant that there was no reason to feel awkward because he was so used to girls throwing themselves at him that another one barely made a difference . . . and she felt even more awkward about it and stopped talking.

"Actually, I wanted to talk —" D said.

"This is me," Sam said, interrupting, looking up at a very tall building that wasn't her building at all. Her building was about twenty blocks north of this building. . . .

"This is you?" he said, looking at the building behind her.

"Yup! Well, thanks for walking me home."

"Oh, um, sure. I'll see you tomorrow, I suppose."

"Yup!" Sam waited for him to walk away, but he waited for her to get inside safely (really, *safely* at four-thirty?), so she smiled, waved a little, and walked toward the doorman.

She made a really strange face at the doorman, which she hoped D couldn't see, and he opened the door for her and she stepped inside, waved again, and D nodded and began walking up the street.

When he was far enough away that he was out of her line of sight, Sam stuck her head outside and the doorman said, "He's gone, miss."

"Oh," Sam said, straightening. "Thank you."

"No problem, miss," the tall man said, straightening the front of his uniform and readjusting his hat before opening the door for her. "May I assist you with anything else?"

"Oh, no, thank you again," Sam said.

The doorman nodded, and Sam snuck out of the building where she absolutely did not live and walked up the street alone this time.

D stood inside the small grocery a few blocks away from where he left Samantha and fiddled with the cash machine while he kept his eyes locked on the sidewalk in front of him. He had to move eventually, when a little old lady asked if he was going to marry the ATM machine or just get money from it. He apologized and stepped away, but not before he saw a familiar red head bobbing up the sidewalk.

He waited a few moments more and then stepped out onto the sidewalk to follow her. They walked, about half a block apart, for another six blocks until Sam walked into a building where she was warmly greeted by the doorman and didn't come back out again (D knew; he waited for another fifteen minutes to be sure).

Did she really want to avoid him so much that she pretended to live in a different building? It's not like D was going to stalk her! Well, not much more than he was doing right now anyway.

When it seemed ridiculous to stay watching her building any longer (well, it was really ridiculous fifteen minutes ago, but who is to judge?) D turned and continued walking uptown toward his own place.

#8 LEARN HOW TO DEAL WITH THINGS IN A MORE PRODUCTIVE MANNER

Samantha was sitting in a very squished booth in a diner by Columbia University with Riley and Brendan. The place was crowded during the breakfast rush with college students who were enjoying being college students; they were talking about interesting things and they seemed so . . . grown-up. The whole thing made Sam want to go home and work on her writing sample so that she too could be grown-up and sit in a diner with crappy food and be talking about writing with her fellow UCLA writing students. It never occurred to Sam that she wouldn't get into the writing program, but as time went by it became clearer and clearer that she might end up being just another nameless freshman in the nameless UCLA crowd.

She could barely concentrate on what Riley and Brendan were talking about, and she was sure that she had probably already agreed to more than one thing that she would regret later.

"What's that?" Sam asked, pointing at the bright orange folder that Riley had pulled out of her bag.

Riley folded up the edge so that Sam couldn't see the contents of the folder, but she waggled her eyebrows in a way that was seriously getting on Sam's nerves. "These, my dear friend, are the printouts from all the guys who want to be your date to the Spring Fling."

"What did she just say?" Sam asked Brendan.

"I have no idea, but we've already confirmed four e-mails. Except two are from freshmen, so I don't know if we are even counting those."

Obviously Samantha should have been paying closer attention to the conversation. "Wait, hold up! Go back, what are these e-mails, who are they from . . . and how do they know me?"

Riley rolled her eyes. "I just told you, after we talked, I posted a note on my Facebook page — don't worry, it was private — that said that you were looking 'for a Spring Fling date and that if anyone was interested, they should e-mail."

"Ugh," Sam said, slumping in her seat, causing her hot tea to slosh over the side a little. Brendan quickly dabbed at the mess with his napkin and then, having no place to put the wet napkin, tucked it behind the ketchup and sugar canister. "One, how did you make it private?"

"Well, I made it for Curtis Prep students only — CP has their own Facebook group — so I just linked it —"

"I don't need all the details," Sam said, covering her face with her hands and putting her forehead on the table. "So, the entire student body thinks I'm a desperate loser?"

"Not the entire student body," Brendan said helpfully. "A bunch replied."

Sam picked her head up to look at him.

"Of course, we've only confirmed four were serious."

Sam's eyes bugged out of her head.

"So far," Riley was quick to add. "Only confirmed four so far. But I know more than four were really interested."

"I don't even know four guys who go to Curtis Prep!" Sam cried. "I can't go out with some guy who doesn't even know what I look like."

Riley looked off into the distance, at a space right above Sam's left shoulder. Sam shifted in her seat until Riley had no choice but to look her in the eyes.

"I might have added a picture."

"What picture?"

"A good one!" Riley assured her.

"Yeah, it was!" Brendan said, nodding emphatically.

"Don't help," Riley muttered under her breath. "Anyway, there's a picture and a really well-written description — I wrote it — and it's . . . Samantha, stop hitting your head against the table."

"This is so ridiculous! I'm going to be the laughingstock of the entire school."

"You are not!" Brendan cried. "Seriously, this is such a great idea. I'm definitely going to try this when we're done. Samantha, seriously, stop. People are watching."

Sam picked up her head and saw there was a group of college boys at the table next to them, staring at her like she was crazy. She smiled and waved at them, and one kid nodded, but the rest just went back to picking at their omelets and French toast.

Sam eyed the orange folder. Orange began to take on new meaning to Sam. No longer just a color, it now represented all that was wrong with the world. This orange folder was the end of her social life (before it even had a chance to begin!). She needed that folder; she *wanted* that folder.

"Can I see . . ." Sam asked, reaching for it.

Riley snapped it back. "No, that would prejudice our opinion of each candidate unduly."

"What is she talking about?" Sam asked Brendan.

Brendan looked at Riley in an assessing way. "I think," he said, turning to Sam, "that she wants us to discuss them before you give any input so that way it is fair and impartial."

"She thinks this is fair and impartial? She knows all these people, I don't!"

"I don't know *all* of them," Riley said. "I certainly don't know the freshmen. You're not interested in dating a freshman, are you?"

"I don't know," Sam said. "Can I look at the e-mails?"

Riley thought about it for a moment. "No, I don't think so."

Sam screamed a frustrated cry, just as the waitress appeared to see if they needed anything. She hurried off while Riley made "Don't worry, she's only a little crazy" hand signals.

SAM GETS MORE DATES THAN D CAN HANDLE

Brynna, D's housekeeper and de facto parent, placed a tray of mini English muffin pizzas on a plate in the middle of the large wooden kitchen table. Brendan grabbed two, Riley was too busy playing with an ominous-looking orange folder, and Marley glanced at the food only long enough to sneer, and then went back to looking bored.

"She totally has to go out with this Walker kid," Riley said, pulling a page out of the folder and passing it around the table.

By the time it reached D, he already hated the kid. Whoever he was. Even Marley looked interested by what she was reading; when she passed the paper to D, he practically ripped it out of her hands.

Marley just raised her eyebrows. D told her to shut up and looked at the page.

It said:

RED: lovely color
of my lips when I finish
playing the trombone.

Red hair and freckles
do warm this trombone player's
heart. Go out with me?

I will serenade
you with my trombone.

I'll add something . . .
It will be a lovely tune.

Oh! New red-haired girl —
Will you please go out with me?
I play the trombone.

D snorted. "I think he plays the trombone."

"Can you tell a girl that you are going to 'serenade' her with your 'trombone'?" Brendan asked, plucking the paper out of D's hands while shoving an entire English muffin pizza into his mouth.

"She should totally go out with him," Riley said, marking the e-mail with a big smiley face.

"No, she shouldn't. I don't think all these haikus are *really* haikus."

The four of them had decided to meet without Samantha present, so they could go over the initial e-mails, which were already up to twenty.

"Twenty?" Marley said. "Twenty boys want to date her?"

"I'm so doing this next," Brendan said. "Hey, do you have anything to drink?"

D jerked his head toward the cabinet. Brendan got up and opened it. "Um, I didn't mean alcohol. Do you have anything else?"

D shrugged, and Brendan went to the fridge and pulled out a bottle of water. D wasn't sure why they were all in his apartment ("For privacy!" Riley had said, like this was a freakin' state secret), but now he wanted them all to go. And he wanted the orange folder to stay. He wanted to introduce the orange folder to the wonderful gas-powered fireplace in his living room.

"So, how should we go through them?" Riley asked the group.

"I think we should just read and rank them, then the lowest ones go."

Everyone pulled out pens and started going through the applications. There were one or two that were no-brainers.

The ones that should automatically be crossed off the list: the girls, for one.

"I think this Walker kid should get nixed," D said.

"Write it down and shut up, I'm trying to read," Marley mumbled, pulling the cap of her red pen off with her teeth.

"No, I like Walker!" Riley cried, snatching the paper from D's hands and scribbling out the big zero that he had written at the top of the page.

"He's stalking her. With bad haikus," D said after a moment of hesitation, realizing that the freshman was stalking her with haikus, but he was actually stalking her. Well, not at the moment.

"They weren't so bad," Brendan said.

"They were trombone haikus. This kid is obviously crazy."

"Or he's obviously a trombone player," Riley said.

"Is there anything obvious about a trombone player?" Brendan asked.

"Oh, I thought that whole trombone thing was just a euphemism," Marley said, tilting her head and looking confused.

"He's out," D said.

"In," the other three responded, and D crumbled. But when the others looked down at their papers, he snuck a small smile. This was going to be easier than he thought: As long as he could keep the dating pool to freshman trombone players (who wrote haikus), he had absolutely nothing to worry about.

Samantha had the phone hooked under her ear, against her shoulder, and was lying on her stomach crosswise on her bed while trying to write her new sample pages. It just wasn't working; nothing she came up with sounded any less trite and boring than the other sample (the other billion samples) that she had already written.

She snapped the notebook shut, sending three pencils flying.

Riley was rattling off something about her first date in her ear, in the midst of stories about Eric and about this really great pair of shoes that she wanted to buy but couldn't figure out what color to get, so she just got both . . . and did she mention that one of Sam's dates was with a freshman?

"I'm not going to get arrested, am I?" Sam asked.

"Of course not. Wait . . . when do you turn eighteen?" Riley asked.

"Not until the end of the summer."

"Oh! Then you're fine. . . ." Riley said, making Samantha cringe. "We picked two already and we're still getting more e-mails!

"Yeah," Riley continued, "I think what we'll do is that you'll come over here and they can pick you up and then they can drop you off here and you can give all of us —"

"All of us?"

"Yeah, you know, all of us . . . Brendan . . . D . . . Marley . . . Well, after each of your dates you can come back here and tell us about it and we can then rate your dates based on your enjoyment — both obvious and subtle — and how cute we think the two of you look together."

Samantha wondered what D thought about this whole operation. Was he as worried about it as she was or was D just happy to have her off his hands? If she had a date for the dance, he wouldn't have to worry about it. He could even ask someone else to go. . . .

"Was that your idea?"

"No, Brendan's . . . We can't have you walking around with someone who looks totally inappropriate for you."

"Would it be more important to see if someone *feels* more inappropriate, and isn't that something I could judge for myself?"

"Samantha, darling," Riley said softly. "If that was the case, would we be in this position to begin with?"

"I guess I see your point."

They said their good-byes, with plans for Samantha to go over to Riley's house in two nights (on a Thursday!) for her first date. She wasn't told who she was going out with, or what they would be doing, but she knew he was expected at six-thirty, so Sam had to be at Riley's house at six P.M.

Samantha, not for the first time, wanted to bow out of the whole thing, but something (and it was D, she knew it) kept her from calling the whole thing off. Instead she decided that she would stick it out. I mean, what was the worst thing that could happen? Three dates, and then a date for the dance . . . how bad could it be?

D TRIES TO KEEP SAM FROM GETTING BUSY

It was Thursday evening and D was sitting in Riley's living room, where her stepmother was passing out drinks to everyone. D took a sip of his and made a horrible face.

"Too sour?" Riley asked.

"What is this?"

"Lemonade," Riley answered, Marley and Brendan looking on.

"Virgin?"

"D's not used to virgins, Riley," Marley said from the opposite side of the room, where she had plopped herself into one of the large striped chairs. Brendan was sitting on the Oriental rug, his legs crossed underneath him while he pulled organic snacks that his mother had packed for him out of his bag, stuffing them unceremoniously into his mouth while he chuckled, spewing small bits of crumbs all over the front of his shirt.

D glared at Marley, who didn't even look up from the magazine she was flipping through.

Ever since last year, when Marley broke up with her

boyfriend, she had been acting like such a bitch. It wasn't D's fault that he had encouraged her boyfriend to dump Marley, using the irrefutable logic "You're only young once, right?" And Marley's boyfriend dumped her to go make out with some freshman girls and ever since . . . well, whatever "friendship" Marley and D might have been acting like they had, had considerably cooled.

"Come on, guys," Riley said. "Sam is going to be here any moment and we all have to come together."

D sat down on the couch opposite of Marley and looked over his shoulder at Riley standing behind them. He held the lemonade gingerly in his hand, waiting for someone (anyone) else to take a sip so he could see if they thought it tasted funny too. It *had* been a long time since he had lemonade, but . . . was it supposed to taste like carburetor fluid?

The doorbell rang and Riley ran to fetch Samantha, and when Sam walked in, she was carrying a purse in one hand and lemonade in the other. Attack of the hospitable step-mother.

"Hey, guys," she said, looking around for a place to set her drink or her bag. She found neither and then awkwardly juggled them for a second before D stood, crossing to her, and held her drink for her. She shot him a grateful look and was able, with one hand, to take off her light coat and throw it over the back of a chair.

"You look nice, Sam," Riley said.

D thought she looked better than nice. She had left her hair down and hadn't overdone the makeup, and she was wearing a simple black skirt that cut right around her knees — and a tight black shirt that showed off her curves. And what curves they were.

D turned away and took a big sip of his lemonade, his eyes watering as he tried to swallow it.

"Thanks," he heard Sam say from behind him. He had to bite the inside of his cheek and swallow really, really slowly to keep from gagging. He looked around; nobody else had taken a sip of their lemonade. Maybe this was a big trick — he looked around for cameras.

"So, are you ready for your first date, Sam?" Marley called out from the chair.

"Um, this isn't my *first* date, Marley."

"Whatever," she said, waving Samantha's answer off with her hand — the same way one would to a bug that was buzzing around your head.

"Oh, this is going to be so much fun!" Brendan sighed. "And you look beautiful. Are you going to kiss him good night?"

D waited for the answer.

"Um, I think I'd like to figure out who I am going out with before I figure out if there is going to be a good-night kiss," Sam said slowly, as if speaking to a small child. And judging from the way Brendan's face looked to D, he thought that the approximation was about right. Brendan pouted. Brendan was, after all, a romantic.

"So, are you going to tell me who my first date is?"

"Absolutely," Riley said, pulling out her folder. D wondered if she had started carrying that thing around with her everywhere, because the outside had phone numbers, homework assignments, and a shopping list written on it. It looked like it had been "the only thing on hand" during a few points where Riley had needed to remember something.

Riley pulled out her iPhone and read the name off:

"Joshua Cole."

"Wow, that's great," Samantha said, clearly not knowing who Joshua Cole was. D smiled. Joshua Cole was one of his favorites — if by favorites you could mean that Joshua Cole was one of the most obnoxious, most pretentious jerks in the entire school. But he hadn't dated Marley (or Brendan), and Riley didn't know him, so D was able to give him a big thumbs-up that the others couldn't deny.

D almost felt bad for a second — he figured that he had ensured that Samantha would be having an absolutely crappy date. And then when he, D, asked her out, she'd be so happy to have a date with someone normal that she'd say yes and never even think of going out with anyone else.

And it wasn't like he wasn't punishing himself at the same time: He would be spending the next two and a half hours sitting at Riley's house with Marley and Brendan, while Samantha was on a date. Even with a kid like Joshua, it was still a date, and D had to tell himself to consciously relax lest he get overexcited and tip off the others to what his real game was.

Riley guided Samantha to a love seat that had been pulled away from its usual place by the wall and sat her down, patting her shoulders as she did so.

"He'll be here in five minutes and then I can formally introduce you." Riley smiled and Samantha cringed.

Four minutes and twenty-three seconds later, the doorbell rang again, and another fifteen seconds after that, Riley returned to the living room with a boy in tow.

D sized up Joshua Cole as he walked in. He looked normal enough. He was wearing jeans, sneakers, and a sweater that D would swear was stolen off the set of *Mister Rogers' Neighborhood*. But otherwise, he looked like an average teenage guy — which was a key part of the plan, so nobody else would be questioning his initial decision — but D knew that the minute he started talking . . . then it would get interesting.

Riley smiled at Joshua and then at Samantha, waggling her eyebrows and rolling her eyes in Joshua's direction. Joshua turned to Samantha on the love seat and his smile broadened. He walked over to her and shook her hand, kissing her on the cheek and presenting her with a flower.

"At least it isn't a rose," Marley mumbled. It was an orchid. A wilting one.

Riley sighed as Samantha said thank you and Joshua nodded.

D laughed, in spite of himself: Joshua wasn't talking. Nobody had noticed either. But Joshua hadn't said a word since he got there. This was going to be so great.

"OK, let's get the formalities out of the way so that the two of you kids can go out and enjoy your date!" Riley said. "First of all, I'd like you to both observe some rules: There will be no physical interaction beyond first base." (D could see Sam turn bright red, but this was his addition to the rules and he thought it was and should be mandatory.) "You will have her back here by eight forty-five exactly, and you will pay for everything." (This had been Riley's stipulation, as she still believed if they were going dutch they might as well be going to different places.)

They both nodded, although Sam looked like she wanted to burst into tears.

"Great!" Riley said. "Brendan will now introduce you to your date."

Brendan jumped up, smiling at the both of them, and took the sheet of paper from Riley's hands. "Hi, guys. I'm Brendan." (He didn't need to introduce himself; everyone knew who he was.) "Hi." (He waved at everyone in the room.) "So, like, this is so great. And I'm so glad everyone is here. And I think this is great."

He smiled again. D wanted to hit him.

"Anyway," he said, crisping the paper in his hands. "Um, meet Samantha Owens." (He waved a little at Sam, D groaned,

Sam smiled and waved back.) "Sam is a seventeen-year-old senior. She likes reading and tortoises. She has a younger brother and recently moved back to Manhattan from her boarding school." He paused, read it over again to himself, and then nodded. And then said, "Hi, Sam."

"Um, hi, Brendan."

Then Brendan flipped over the page, and it was all D could do to keep from laughing. "Joshua Cole is really interested in business management. His parents promised him a new car if he gets an eight hundred on the verbal portion of the SATs next month. He really wants this car." Brendan flipped the page over, and over again, and then, deciding there was nothing more to read, looked up and said, "Um, hi, Joshua."

Joshua nodded and looked around. Still no speaking. It was all D could do to keep from laughing.

Sam, in order to avoid the rest of what was happening, took a deep sip of her lemonade and, half a second later, her face froze and she began coughing. There was much coughing.

"Ugh, what is this?" she asked.

"I know, right?" D asked.

Marley looked at them both, took a long sip, and then went back to her magazine. Riley looked at both D and Sam in a chiding manner and then realized that she wanted to finish things fast, before they completely fell apart, and pushed both Sam and Joshua out of the room before another word was spoken.

"Have fun, you two!" she called out.

After she had shut the door behind them, she sat looking quizzically at the others.

Marley stood up and grabbed the application. "*Amo . . . amas . . .* What the hell?! Is this English?"

"Marley," Riley said, ripping the application out of her hand, "it's Latin."

"He wrote his application in Latin? What, why?" Marley asked.

"From what I can tell, his parents thought Latin classes would help him excel on the SATs and, if his application is to be believed, if he takes these classes seriously and scores above a seven hundred, they are going to buy him a new car," Riley said. "Or a pig."

"Huh?"

"I had to type the entire application into the Latin-English translator. Some of it wasn't exactly directly translatable." She put the application back in her folder. What D wouldn't give for five minutes with that folder.

"So, how is Sam supposed to talk to him if he is only speaking in Latin?" Brendan asked.

"I don't think he's only speaking in Latin, Brendan."

And if he was? Riley must've sensed Brendan's unuttered question because she quickly finished with: "Just think of it like a date with a foreign exchange student. They can use body language. I once went out with Val, the foreign exchange student from freshman year, and we had so much in common even though we couldn't understand one word the other one was saying."

"She shouldn't have to use body language, he speaks ENGLISH," Marley said. "Whose date idea was this anyway?"

"Er . . ." D said.

"It was D's," Riley said, checking the paperwork.

"I think it'll be good for her to broaden her dating horizons," he said, willing everyone to drop it. Riley looked at him with a very suspicious look on her face. D tried to smile as charmingly as possible. Two hours and fourteen minutes left until Sam was back. D tried to stifle his smile. It couldn't come too soon — probably for either of them.

#9 LEARN TO SPEAK AN EXOTIC NEW LANGUAGE AND VISIT AN EXOTIC NEW PLACE

Samantha did not think there was going to be a second date with Joshua Cole. She was pretty sure he felt the same way.

It started when they got into the cab. He held the door, which was a nice touch, but then they only drove two blocks. They couldn't have walked two blocks? Sam tried to ask Joshua about it, but when he didn't know enough Latin to answer properly, he would shake his head violently and shoot her really pissed-off glares.

Sam finally asked, "So . . . what's with the Latin?"

Joshua took a beaten-up index card out of his back pocket and handed it to her. Sam looked at it, trying to decipher the extremely small print.

"You get a scar if you get a perfect score?"

He shook his head and pantomimed.

"Oh, a car," she said, nodding slowly. "I don't get it. Do you really need a car in Manhattan?"

He did not look pleased. Instead of answering (in Latin or otherwise), he simply ripped the card from her hands and looked out the window, sulking.

They got out of the cab and Josh walked her to the front door: not to a restaurant or even a movie theater, but to his apartment. She knew so, because the doorman greeted him by name and looked at her like she was crazy for following Josh "Latin Boy" Cole up to his den of darkness.

Sam, obviously, felt the same way.

Sam did not feel like she was on a date with a foreign exchange student. She felt like she was on a date with an idiot. And she was in the idiot's apartment and, from the looks of it, about to have dinner with the idiot's parents.

Sam walked into a poorly lit apartment that would have made Riley cry. The space wasn't very small, but all the furniture was so huge that it obscured any sense of scale in the space. The walls were all painted dark colors, which added to the smallness of it all, and Sam was pretty sure that if she would ever have an attack of claustrophobia, this would be the time for it to happen.

The entire apartment reminded her of her old Nana's basement. It even smelled about the same.

Despite that, she tried to keep an open mind as Joshua introduced her to his parents (at least that's what she thought he did). Sam thought it was a bit early to be meeting the parents, but for all she knew, Joshua always had his parents join in on a first date. It's not like she could ask him (or understand his answer, rather).

His parents were both lawyers, who spent the majority of the meal e-mailing each other across the table, things that they both thought were amusing. Joshua kept his eyes on his plate.

When either addressed Samantha, from the other side of a rather long wooden table that sat impressively (and alone) in a long room that if it had been any narrower would've been a hallway, they did so in short, clipped sentences — often referring to each other as "Joshua's father" or "Joshua's mother."

"Would you like some more peas, Samantha? I can have Joshua's mother pass them to you."

It was awkward. It was more than awkward, it was terrifying. Samantha wanted to go home. When dinner was over, both of Joshua's parents got up from the table without a farewell and a cook brought out two puddings that were placed in front of both of the kids.

"*Vis efficere?*"[1] he asked.

"No, thank you," Samantha said, looking at her bowl. "This is quite enough."

---

1. "Want to make out?"

She couldn't understand why Joshua pouted through dessert; it was quite delicious.

Joshua tried to make conversation, but it was really hard to follow — it being a dead language and all. But she tried to remember a few bits that she could look up later.

Like when she asked what he wanted to do, and he responded with *"Fallit me."*[2] Or when he tried to put his hand on her leg under the table and she pushed him firmly away and his only response (after rolling his eyes) was: *"Id faciunt omnes."*[3]

When she finally got tired of trying to figure out what he was saying through reading his body language (which only went from being standoffish to outright pouting), Sam finally yelled, "Can you just stop talking in Latin?"

"Vah! Denoune Latine loquor? Me ineptus — interdum modo abit."[4]

She spent the rest of their "date" watching television with Joshua's mother while Josh pouted in his room, where she was pretty sure she sneaked a peek of him playing World of Warcraft on his PC.

When it was time for him to bring her back to Riley's, he stepped out of the building and went to hail a cab.

---

2. "I don't know."
3. "Everyone's doing it." (Latin peer pressure)
4. "Oh! Was I speaking Latin again? Silly me — sometimes it just sort of slips out."

"Um, couldn't we just walk? It's, like, two blocks," Sam asked, pointing down the street.

Joshua rolled his eyes and shrugged, following her slowly down the sidewalk. When they were standing on Riley's stoop, and Samantha was sure she felt someone looking out the window at them (Riley), she said in as friendly a manner as she could, "It was really nice getting to know you and your family, Joshua. I hope you do very well on your SATs."

Joshua responded, "*Noli me vocare, ego te vocabo.*"[5]

She smiled and Joshua hailed a cab going back up the street (two blocks) and once he seemed a safe enough distance away, Samantha was buzzed into the building. When she went to ring Riley's doorbell, the door was ripped open before her finger really even had a chance to touch the button.

"How was it?" Riley cried. D stood next to her, looking Sam up and down as if waiting for a reaction.

"Can I at least keep my humiliation to myself until I get inside?" she asked, pushing past Riley and walking into the living room where the other two waited patiently. She thought she saw a knowing look on D's face, but when she glanced back, it was gone and she figured she imagined the whole thing.

So Samantha told them all about the date, including the Latin she could remember (which Brendan Googled on his iPhone, while mumbling that he knew he should've gotten that

---

5. "Don't call me, I'll call you."

Latin translator application), and all in all they were all very disappointed by Samantha's first date.

"Well, I hope you didn't sleep with him," Marley said.

"Of course not, his parents were there," Brendan said, turning around to look at Marley.

"So?" she asked.

"Eh. I'm not sleeping with any boy who can't even hold a conversation with me!" Samantha said, and the minute she did, she saw D physically tense up. *Good*, she thought.

Riley nodded. "Samantha's right! The next boy should be eloquent and well versed in the art of communicating his feelings. In English."

"Oh god, I hope that wasn't a hint," Samantha cried.

"Monday night, next date. Be here at five."

"I have homework!" Samantha cried.

"Five-thirty, then," she said magnanimously. "The rest of you too."

The "meeting" was adjourned and the group split up, Riley staying home to call her boyfriend and watch reality television, Marley to go do something that was probably illegal in most states, Brendan to go do whatever Brendan did . . . and D . . . D waited for Samantha.

D LEARNS THAT HE DOESN'T LIKE LATIN EITHER

D excused himself to use Riley's bathroom, so that he could wait out Marley's and Brendan's departure. Once he heard them leave and only Sam's and Riley's voices were left, he washed his hands and walked out of the bathroom.

"Hey," D said, walking up to Samantha. "Can I walk you home?"

"Sure," Samantha said after a moment of hesitation, glancing at Riley, who just smiled and kissed them both on the cheeks and wished them a safe and wonderful walk home. If she didn't do it in a really annoying singsong voice, it wouldn't have been so obvious. But D figured that's what best friends were for.

D didn't push his luck and just smiled and walked in front of her, backward, while he talked: "Did he really make you take a cab two blocks?"

Sam nodded.

"And you had dinner with his parents?"

Sam nodded again.

"And —"

"Ugh, I can't take it anymore! No more talking about it!" Sam cried. "If I hear one more word about Joshua Cole, I will not only scream but I will swear off men forever!"

D stopped and Samantha, not paying attention to him, bumped into him — chest first. D steadied her. "That would be a shame," he said, then he pulled her coat around her tightly, because it was chilly out — or because she shivered — and smiled before taking a step back. For a moment D wanted to say something important, except he had no idea what to say. All that tumbled through his mind was *Kiss her. Kiss her. Kiss her.*

"Yeah," she said, then lightly shook her head. "What?"

He just smiled and said, "Let's go, tiger. . . . Let's get you home."

The next morning, as D was leaving gym class, he overheard a nasal voice, normally reserved for Latin only, talking to another student. And while D didn't want to be overly worried, the fact that Joshua was speaking English was enough to cause D to pause and listen to what was being said.

"That girl was such a bitch," D overheard Joshua saying to another student he didn't recognize. D didn't want to get mad over nothing; perhaps he was talking about someone else.

"Seriously, who needs to take applications to find a date anyway? She's seriously twisted."

That was enough for D. He stepped out from behind the lockers, noting with satisfaction the look of surprise (and then mistrust) on Joshua's face.

"What's up, Hammond?" Joshua asked him.

"Not much, Cole. But I heard you speaking about my friend Samantha."

"What's it to you?"

"Like I just said, she's my friend. Do you need me to repeat it in Latin?"

"Blow off, Hammond."

"It's just that if you were saying something bad about my friend, I'd have to teach you a lesson about how to properly treat a lady. And we both know that it would be a shame, considering what a lame prick you are."

"*Quid me appellavisti?!?!*"[6] Joshua's face turned bright red and he kept clenching and unclenching his fists.

"Shall we go outside?" D asked, rolling up his sleeves.

---

6. "What did you call me?"

Samantha was sitting in the library during lunch that day when Justin put his hands over her eyes and told her to "Guess who."

For a second she thought it was D and her heart did a pitter-pat and her stomach did a somersault, but when she turned around, she couldn't hide the look of disappointment on her face.

"Wasn't who you were expecting, huh?" Justin laughed, sitting on the edge of the table Samantha was working on.

"I wasn't expecting anyone."

"Just wished it was someone else?"

Samantha didn't have a response for that, so she decided it was safer to just not say anything at all.

"This isn't about a certain guy with a certain accent, is it?" Justin asked. Samantha was unable to keep herself from turning a brilliant shade of pink, and Justin simply nodded.

"Can I tell you something about D?"

Samantha wanted to say no, she didn't want to hear anything bad about D, but she found herself nodding, because really, she wanted to hear about him. She wanted to talk about him. She . . . wanted him.

"He loves the chase, you know?" Justin said, standing and pacing around and behind Samantha's chair. "If you're too easy, he'll lose interest."

"I wouldn't consider myself *too easy*," Sam said, bristling.

"No, no, that's not what I mean. Just don't let him know you're available, make him work for it a little."

"Easier said than done," Samantha said. "I mean, that's making an assumption that he's actually interested in me."

"Oh, he's interested," Justin said, his eyes sparkling.

Samantha tried to pretend *she* wasn't interested but she could barely keep her voice level as she asked, "Oh, how do you know that?"

"Maybe because he just beat the crap out of the Latin King."

"Joshua Cole?"

"The very same."

"Why?" Samantha asked, generally confused. Had Joshua said something in Latin that D took offense to?

"Why do you think?" Justin asked, watching Samantha very carefully. "You know, there is absolutely nothing that would drive D as crazy as you going out with me. . . ."

* * *

Samantha was walking to her locker after sixth period on Monday when Riley ran into her and practically slammed her into the wall.

"What the heck?" Sam cried, trying to right herself while Riley hung on her arm.

"Tonight's your second date!" Riley cried.

"Don't remind me," Sam said, spinning the dial on the lock. She opened the door and out fell a card that said: *Go two lockers to the right, the combination is 4-49-1.*

"What's this?" Riley asked, trying to pull the card out of Sam's hands.

"I have no idea."

"Well?"

"It says that I should open the locker two down from mine."

"Well? Do it!"

"I don't know if I should," Samantha said, looking skeptically at the envelope. "Who knows what's in there? Maybe it's a bomb."

"It's not a bomb," Riley said. She plucked the paper from Sam's hand, walked to the locker, and spun the combination. "Ew, it's someone's locker."

"Of course it is. What did you think it would be? A sarcophagus?"

"What's a — oh! A note!" Riley took out a note that was

obviously the same stationery and handwriting. "Open it!" she said, flinging it in Sam's general direction.

Sam opened it and grinned. "It says to walk across the hall and open locker number one thirty-nine . . . and it has a combo here."

They opened the next combo and it said: *Last one, promise. Go to locker #41. Please don't dawdle, I only rented these lockers until the end of the school day.*

They made it to locker #41 and inside there was a photograph of someone's lips, puckered up for a kiss.

"At least I think those are lips."

"Yeah, probably."

"Does this have anything to do with my next date?" Sam asked, waving the picture in front of Riley's face.

"Not that I know of." But Sam thought she looked suspicious.

"Uh-huh."

"Well, um, I'll see you after school!"

D LEARNS THE SUBTLE ART OF LICKING HIS WOUNDS

D was busy serving detention after school when he was supposed to be at Riley's house to see Sam off on her second date and to — as Riley put it — go through some "committee work." Whatever that meant.

Instead he was sitting at a desk in an empty room (empty aside from the fact that Joshua Cole, who was muttering under his breath in Latin, sat two seats away from him — but he was ignoring his presence).

D's right hand hurt, where he had repeatedly smashed it into Joshua's jaw. But Joshua, the little Latin-speaking booger, had managed to bite him on the hand, really hard. In exchange, Joshua was sporting an amazing black eye.

If a bite mark (and probable rabies) wasn't bad enough, D had received an e-mail earlier that afternoon from his father about his college applications. He was expected for dinner, at which point they would be having "a talk."

Great, just what D needed.

#10 LOCK LIPS WITH SOMEONE SPECIAL

Sam was going on her second date. With the lips.

Walker Saunders's lips, to be exact.

The "committee" let them both off easy without any weird introductions or embarrassing episodes, but Sam was so tense that it hardly mattered.

"Where is D?" she asked Riley.

"Detention."

"Oh."

Sam spent the time before her date reading the e-mail that Walker had sent (she was allowed to read it this time) (preparation, Riley had said, was key), and she thought seriously about canceling the whole thing, but Justin's advice kept ringing in her ears. She didn't want to be too obvious about her interest in D. If he needed a little competition, she'd make sure he had it.

She thought about Walker.

There were pros and cons to this choice, as Sam saw it. The pros were: He was cute. He seemed exceedingly sweet. He didn't know Latin. Cons: He was a freshman. And not that there needed to be more cons than that, but the years that divided them seemed like great leaps. He was in the fifth grade when she was in the eighth grade.

She was dating a fifth grader.

Not *dating*. Just going on a date.

She waited in Riley's apartment with the other committee members, who were anxiously waiting for her to leave so they could talk about her third and final date, when Walker showed up.

He was wearing a T-shirt, a hoodie, and shorts. It was way too cold for shorts and Sam couldn't help but wonder why he wasn't dressed more appropriately. Then she chided herself for being "old." And then mentally chided him for being "young."

He said hello to everyone. Riley welcomed him enthusiastically — she hadn't met Walker before, but he knew Brendan from lacrosse — and Marley deigned a faint eyebrow raise when Walker mentioned he was in some classes with her younger sister. Then she did what she always did: She went back to reading a magazine. (Marley actually just scanned the pages, not as if she was inputting any text into her cranium. It was mostly staring at pictures and folding down the corners for the pages that had items she'd like to buy. But, for Marley, we will count this as reading.)

Sam took a good look at her date for the evening. He *was* kinda cute. He looked more like a football player than a musician. He was a big kid.

Guy, she meant. Guy.

When Walker was introduced to Samantha, he gave her a hug and said it was nice to meet her, and Samantha felt herself melt a little. He was still a freshman, but he was a charming little bugger.

They left on their date.

On the 4 train, going downtown, Walker asked her questions about herself (in English), about her time in upstate New York, about how she felt about moving to Manhattan. He told her that he admired the guts it took to do something so big and drastic before the end of high school, while Samantha blushed and thought about how mature Walker was. For a kid.

She told him about writing and he told her about his trombone.

The conversation was pleasant, if a little inane.

They went to see a movie in Times Square, and when Sam was sure that Walker was going to pick the one comedy that she knew her younger brother wanted to see (Oh god, Walker was the same age as her brother. She was dating her brother!), he surprised her by asking what she had seen and then arguing over the merits of what movies neither of them had seen yet. They opted for the new Bond movie. Walker leaned over about midway through the movie and told her how much he hated people who talked all the way through the movie, and then spent the next fifteen minutes doing just that — making Sam laugh over and over.

When the movie was finished, he turned to her and said, "Well, the movie is over but I'm not ready to say good-bye yet." And all she could do was smile and nod.

"Want to grab a bite?" he asked.

"I'd really like that."

So they hopped on the subway to go all the way down to Union Square, where Samantha's favorite diner was (well, the only diner she actually had ever eaten at). They walked into Chat 'n' Chew, a basementlike spot that had all sorts of 1950s kitchen signage nailed into the plank walls and really low ceilings. Walker pretended to be suitably impressed, and Sam was pleased. He ordered a burger, a shake, fries, and rings. Sam ordered a steak salad.

"This place is amazing," he said, looking around at the diner . . . and Samantha felt happy with her choice.

They spent the rest of their time together talking and laughing. She was actually a little nervous because at some point she decided that Walker wasn't such a kid (and not a bad kid) after all and . . . could she date a freshman? And immediately D's face flashed in her memory and she figured it just wouldn't happen.

"What are you thinking about?" Walker asked.

Samantha laughed and blushed and then laughed again. "I was just thinking that I was surprised that I am having so much fun."

Walker pretended to look upset. "Why wouldn't you have fun?"

"Well, I just didn't think we'd have anything in common. You are a . . ."

"A . . . ?"

"Well . . . you're a . . ."

"Trombone player?" Walker added helpfully.

Samantha nodded. "Yes, a trombone player."

Walker nodded in what appeared to be a very sage manner. "Yes, I get that a lot."

"You do?"

"Yes, I date girls all the time who are more used to guitar players or drummers, but let me tell you, the trombone is more than an instrument. It's a way of life."

"Oh?" Samantha asked, leaning forward, her arms resting on the table.

"Yup," he said, twirling his straw in his glass.

"Can you expand on that?"

"Have you ever played a trombone?"

"Can't say that I have."

"Well, you hold it like this," Walker said, pantomiming holding a trombone. "And it takes much more air than a lot of the small brass instruments, a steady stream of air. So you're constantly forced to really identify what your body is doing and how you are expending your energies. Y'know? So you have to be in tune with yourself."

"OK . . ."

"Not to mention tonguing notes."

"Pardon?"

"When you change notes, to hit the note directly, you push out a strong, steady stream of air but reinforce that with a tongue movement."

Sam shook her head.

"Here, give me your hand," Walker said, getting up and moving to the other side of the booth and nudging her inside. They were both sitting on the same side now, squished onto the red seats. Walker took her left hand and put it over his mouth.

His lips felt soft and dry.

"Now tell me if you can feel this." He blew a steady stream of warm air against the palm of her hand, and every few seconds it would almost stop and start again, and she felt it.

"I feel that."

"That's what goes through the horn when you are tonguing it."

Samantha was starting to get nervous when he kept throwing the term "tonguing" around. "I heard somewhere that trombone players are good kissers," she said, trying to make a joke between the tonguing and the haikus he had left for her.

But instead of laughing, he smiled an "I'm not really laughing" smile and then got up and went back to the other side of the table.

Wow, Samantha thought. But she tried to shake it off. Maybe he just didn't get the joke. "It's like your haikus, you know? Trombone players are good kissers . . . ?"

Walker smiled politely and asked for the check.

"Do you want to go somewhere for dessert?" Sam asked.

"Actually, I told Riley I'd have you back by eight-thirty and it's almost nine. . . ."

It wasn't "late" a few minutes ago.

"I mean," he said, "there is a lot of traffic on the subway at this time of night and I wouldn't want to get you home late."

Samantha nodded and followed Walker down into the subway. While she stood with her back against one of the support beams, Walker paced up and down the platform in striding steps, his head hanging over the edge while he looked for the train.

"I don't think that will help it come any faster," Samantha said.

Walker didn't hear or didn't care. When the train finally came and they both boarded, Sam built up some courage and said, "Did I say something wrong? I mean, I thought we were having a really fun time."

"Yeah, totally," Walker said, but he sounded distracted.

"Um, OK . . ."

About two minutes of uncomfortable silence passed before she spoke again. "Riley, me, and a few other people are going to see a comedy show next week. Would you want to join us?"

Walker seemed like he was battling for an answer for a few minutes, and then finally, as his face crumbled, he leaned closer to Sam and said, "I don't want to hurt your feelings; you seem like a really nice girl. I just don't think we're a good fit."

To say that Samantha was shocked would have been an understatement.

"Um, OK," she said.

"It's not that you're not pretty, you're OK," he said. (OK?) "It's just that I take my trombone really seriously and I don't like how you made fun of me for it. I mean, what do you do that is in any way special?"

"Well, I write. . . ."

"Yeah, but I mean, that's just something you do. Trombone is something I live, and you made fun of me for it," Walker said, pouting.

"I didn't make fun of your trombone! I just said that trombone players are good kissers."

"Yeah, that's the other thing. I don't like promiscuous girls."

"Pardon?"

"I mean, maybe you're not promiscuous, but this is our first date and I don't like to move that fast."

"But YOU are the one who left me all those haikus!"

"Those were just haikus, Sam, they didn't *mean* anything."

And that's when Sam realized that even charming freshman boys could be total and complete jerks.

On their way uptown, Sam pretended to ignore Walker, but it didn't quite sink in. Walker just shrugged, pulled out his iPod, and put his earpieces in. So while Sam sat fuming, Walker bopped to the tunes.

When it was her stop, Walker just waved (without removing his earphones) and as she was getting off the train, she kicked him (accidentally, really hard) in the shin.

Sam texted Riley and said she was going straight home. Riley texted back:

Everything OK?

But Sam just ignored it. How could a date that didn't even mean anything still leave her feeling so crappy?

She began thinking that all of this was just a big load of crap . . . going out with other guys when all she really wanted was to go out with D. And in a moment of inspiration (or insanity), she texted D to see if he was around, awake, and available.

Less than thirty minutes later, they were sitting in a bar on the Upper West Side. D had used his fake ID to buy them each a beer. No one was really paying attention (there was some sort of sports game on), but Sam couldn't relax long enough to even take a sip of her first (illegal) drink.

D drank his like it was soda.

"So, the date didn't go well?" D said.

"You know it didn't," Samantha answered.

"Want to talk about it?"

"Absolutely not."

So they didn't. For a few minutes they didn't talk at all, and that was fine. It was nice to sit with D and not talk, or at least it was nice to sit with him and not try to make conversation that never went anywhere.

"You know, I never did like his haikus," D said finally.

Samantha laughed. "I just . . . feel dumb. Y'know?" And D nodded. "I want to experience all these things that I never experienced before, and I want to write and not write boring crap!"

"I'm sure you don't write boring crap," D said, but when Samantha made a face, he let it drop.

"So don't write boring crap."

"Thanks, that's so helpful."

"There's a lot in this city to experience, Samantha," D said, leaning back in his chair. "I'd like to show you the botanical gardens in Brooklyn or an exhibit in a museum or something. I think you'd like stuff like that."

Samantha smiled into her glass as she raised it for a sip. Then quickly put it down again when she smelled it. She really did not like beer.

"Not into beer, huh?"

"No, not at all."

"Why didn't you say something?" D asked, taking the beer away and moving it to the edge of the table.

"I don't know," Samantha said.

"You never have to be afraid to tell me what you think," D said softly. "I want to know you, I want to know what you like."

"I don't like museums. I hate beer," Sam blurted out. "I don't like dating freshmen! And . . ."

"And?" D said, looking a little worried about what would come out next.

"And I want to kiss you."

Samantha blurted it out before she had a chance to say it, but the minute she did, she wanted to take it back. D looked shocked, not upset and not angry. Just shocked.

"Of course, I tried a similar line on my date tonight," Sam said. "And he called me promiscuous."

"Did he, now?" D said, and after a second started to look angry.

"You're not going to beat *him* up too, are you?"

"I don't know what you're talking about," D said, looking around the bar, and then he winked at her.

But he didn't say he was going to kiss her. He didn't say anything about it at all, and Samantha started to feel dumb again. Why could he always make her feel so dumb? It was like he liked her, and flirted with her, but . . . whenever she tried to push it a little further, he pretended that there was nothing else there.

Could that be it, could there be nothing else there?

Samantha was sitting in Starbucks with Riley before school on Thursday. D hadn't shown up again, but she had seen him during the week in school. While he didn't seem standoffish, he certainly didn't seem like he wanted to jump into conversation. But yesterday, she had gotten a text from him that simply said:

I was just thinking about you, so I thought I'd say hi.

Samantha had spent at least forty-five minutes trying to think of something witty or flirty to respond with, and in the end texted:

Hi back.

Which at the time seemed perfect: not too clingy, not too excited, but not not-excited. It was the perfect amount of friendly and cool. Except that he didn't write her another text, so she was forced to spend the rest of the night trying to figure out what she should've said that could've resulted in more conversation. Eventually, at around one in the morning, she threw her phone across the room and told herself it didn't matter because he was probably asleep and she would see him the next day at school. Perhaps even before school.

And that was enough to help her get to sleep.

Except he wasn't there that next morning at Starbucks and instead she had to sit with Riley, who was grilling her about her horrible, torturous, disgustingly putrid date with the boy she had nicknamed Freshman from Hell. FFH, for short. She had been able to avoid Riley and all questions about the date for a few days, but it was time to pay the piper.

And that wasn't the only name she called him, but the rest she only did in her own head.

When Marley and Brendan met them after school, she had to explain the whole thing over again.

"This is why you don't date freshmen," Marley had said. "They can't handle a strong woman who knows what she wants in bed."

Everyone had looked at her in awe — and not the good kind of awe.

"They weren't going to sleep together," Riley said.

"I wasn't going to sleep with him."

"She was, like, half a decade older than him. She could have been his teen-mommy!" Brendan exclaimed as Samantha shot him a dirty look.

Marley simply shrugged and put down her magazine, yawned, and said she was going home. She had an early appointment with her trainer.

"Don't sleep with anyone on your way out," Brendan called after her. "Actually," Brendan continued, after Marley left, "I have to go too — I just didn't want to have to walk out with her. She would've made me pay for her cab ride home." He rolled his eyes, picked up his bag, and kissed both of them on the cheeks before leaving.

What had seemed so horrible a few days ago had a faint sheen of the ridiculous to it. Except she knew that she would never be able to date a freshman again (aw) but mostly because she was sure Walker was going to tell everyone she didn't respect his trombone.

Sam shook her head and tried to forget that last thought.

"What are you shaking your head at?" Riley asked, adjusting the hem of her skirt to cover the tops of her knees as she sat on a deep leather sofa in the corner of the coffeehouse.

"Nothing, not important," Sam said.

"Well, OK, tonight is your last date," Riley said.

"Oh no," Samantha cried. "No more dates! I can't take it."

"Don't be silly. . . ."

"Silly? I dated a guy who refused to speak English with me and then a guy who told me that my interpretation of his trombone haikus made him feel dirty. How am I being silly by trying to protect myself from more of that?"

Riley looked at her friend and after a moment said, "Let's think of the odds."

"Shall we?" Sam asked sarcastically. Riley ignored her sarcasm.

"One — what are the chances of meeting another one of either of those personalities?"

"Slim, hopefully, and nonexistent if I refuse to date until graduate school."

"And what are the odds that you'll meet the man of your dreams right away?"

Sam automatically thought of D and then had to remember that he wasn't who Riley was talking about. When she didn't respond, Riley continued, "Exactly, so you have to get out there, so you don't miss out on Mr. Right because you are too busy avoiding Mr. Wrong."

"I'm not sure that makes any sense."

"Of course it does. It's not my fault if you don't get it." Riley took a sip of her Frappuccino through its big green straw. "Plus, he's picking you up at seven-thirty."

"What? No." No, no, no, no. NO.

"What do you mean, no? You told the committee you would subject — erm, would agree to go on three dates of our choosing. You're going to renege?"

Samantha looked at her, her mouth agape. "Are you serious?"

"Of course."

"I didn't think that the committee had a death wish for me."

"Don't be dramatic, Sam."

"No, seriously, wasn't the entire point of this exercise to find me good dates . . . to get rid of the bad ones ahead of time? If I wanted to go out on a bunch of horrible dates, I'm sure I could've figured that out all on my own."

Riley nodded. "You're right." But Sam wasn't finished yet —

"Really, whose ideas were these . . . because if I didn't know better, I would think that they were planned to get me to never want to date again!"

"Well, I think we did them all by committee. . . ."

"But you didn't even know Walker."

"True."

"And Joshua?"

"D recommended Joshua."

Samantha stopped. D had recommended she go out with Joshua? "Are they friends?" Sam asked.

"Who, D and Joshua?" Riley asked. "Not that I know of."

"Then . . ."

"Why would D recommend him?" Riley finished Sam's thought for her. Now she was looking perplexed.

"Did D recommend Walker?"

"No," Riley said, shaking her head, and Sam was once again confused. Something had seemed like it was starting to make sense and now it didn't again.

"In fact, he was adamantly against it."

"He was?" Sam asked.

"Yeah, he said something about . . ."

"What?"

"About if you dated a freshman, you'd never want to date anyone again. . . ."

The two girls sat in silence for a moment, before Sam took a deep, loud, slurpy sip of her tea.

"You don't think?" Sam asked Riley.

"I absolutely do," Riley said, putting down her cup.

"On purpose?"

"I think that D wanted you to have bad dates."

"Why?" Sam asked.

"Why do you think?" Riley asked, raising her eyebrows in a suggestive way.

"Really?" Sam said, trying (and failing) to hide her pleasure at what Riley was saying.

"Don't sound so pleased, Sam! This is horrible. My committee has been tampered with. Our findings are all false. Obviously I can't let this happen."

"Um . . . you did let it happen. It happened. Happened, happened, happened."

"No, my good name is now at stake and nobody — not even D — is going to ruin that."

"Riley, I don't think your good name is at stake here."

Riley looked over at Sam in an assessing way that made Sam very, very nervous.

"You need to go out on this last date, to clear my name."

"Riley."

"Sam."

"Why is this date going to be any different?"

Riley squared her shoulders and looked Sam directly in the eye. "Because D didn't help pick this one. In fact, he wasn't even around when we discussed it . . . so this will be our litmus test. If this date is horrible, then the committee was a failure. If this date is what I think it will be, we'll know D was up to something and that he's a pain in my ass."

Samantha looked at her friend; she really did look pissed. She was totally stabbing her Frappuccino with her green straw while trying to mix it.

"Fine," Samantha said. "Who am I going out with tonight?"

"Justin."

"Justin?"

"Justin."

"I'm not doing it," Samantha said, standing up and walking toward the entrance.

Riley jumped up and followed her out the door. "Come on, Sam. What's the big deal? He obviously likes you. He asked you out, you said no, he e-mailed!"

"I want to see it," Sam said. "I want to see the e-mail."

"I don't know how I'm supposed to know what it is you want to look at," she said, huffing a little bit, but pulling her folder out of the bag she had on her shoulder. What Sam wouldn't do to get her hands on that folder for five minutes. Three, if she had some privacy. She could be very destructive in a short amount of time. Perhaps eat the papers?

Riley sifted through some of the pages before pulling a sheet out and reading it.

It was blank except for one paragraph:

i respect women. i like women. i like and respect Sam. plus, i already asked her out and she said no. This might be the only way to get her to give me a chance. help?

Sam shrugged. Riley smiled.

"Not bad, huh?" Riley asked.

"Not horrible. I'm not sure why he can't use caps on his *I*s. . . ."

"Don't start overanalyzing his capitalization."

"His *lack* of capitalization, but fine."

"Fine what?"

"Fine, I'll go out with him."

"YAY!" Riley said, jumping up and down and pulling Sam by her sleeves. Sam tried to act calm and not like her friend looked like she was trying to play ring-around-the-rosy with her.

152

"Can we go to school now?"

"Yes," Riley said.

"What should I do about D?" Samantha asked casually.

"Nothing."

"Nothing?"

"No, I'll take care of D," Riley said, with an edge to her voice.

That was what Sam was afraid of.

D . . .

Thursday after school, D texted Samantha because he hadn't seen her at lunch that day, but she didn't respond. When he got home, he texted Riley, to see what she was up to — and to ask, sneakily, where she thought Samantha might be.

Riley responded to his text, thank goodness, and told D he should come over.

By the time he walked into Riley's, he was surprised to see Brendan and Marley already sitting in the living room.

"Oh, hello," he said to everyone, and then to Riley, "I didn't realize we were all 'meeting.'"

"Yup," Riley said, "Samantha had a date tonight."

D had been picking through the candy dish that was on the end table next to the door. At the word "date," he looked up, his hand halfway to his mouth with a peppermint drop.

"Date?"

"Yes," Riley said, sitting on the couch next to Marley and ripping the magazine from her hands. Marley didn't even look up, but reached into her bag for another mag, and began flipping through that one instead. Brendan was sitting on the rug, as usual, texting someone on his iPhone.

"Date?"

Riley looked up. "Yes. Date."

"I didn't think we had another date scheduled," D said slowly, looking to each person — no one except Riley was meeting his gaze.

"We scheduled it during the last date," Riley said. D took a breath.

"OK, so who is it? Reynold? Mark? Stephen?"

"Justin."

"Justin who?"

"Justin-Justin."

"Justin?"

"Justin."

"Can someone please say Justin again?" Marley drawled. "I didn't quite catch it the first billion times."

"Why is she going out with Justin?" D asked.

"He filled out an application," Brendan said.

"He's hot," Marley answered.

D cringed.

"Sam said she wanted to," Riley put in.

D's heart did a little flip-flop hearing that Sam actually wanted to go out with that jerk Justin. Perhaps if D thought about it a little longer or a little harder, he'd realize that he didn't really think Justin was a jerk. He was one of D's friends, after all — but they used to pick up girls together and get drunk together and . . .

"He's absolutely not right for Samantha."

"And why is that?" Riley asked, her eyebrows raised in a way that annoyed D immensely.

"He's all wrong for her. He drinks and makes out with girls and —"

"Does everything you do?"

"Shut up, Marley."

"She's right, though," Riley said.

"Used to do," D said. "Used to do."

Brendan sat up. "D, do you *like* Samantha?"

"Duh, Captain Obvious. Why don't you get the gay-stuffing out from between your ears," Marley snapped.

"I'd rather have gay-stuffing between my ears than half the school between my legs," Brendan snapped back.

"What the heck is gay-stuffing?" Riley asked.

"Can we please keep on topic!" D shouted, and everyone quieted down.

Brendan was the first one to speak up. "D, you like Samantha?"

D thought about it for a second before answering. "Yes."

"Then why didn't you *say* so? Or better yet, why didn't you just ask her out?" Brendan asked.

"Yeah, I have better things to do with my Thursday nights," Marley replied with a yawn.

"Like the football team?" Brendan asked.

"We don't have a football team, Captain."

"Shut up."

"Could both of you shut up," Riley said to Brendan and Marley. Both of them had the grace to look embarrassed and down at their feet. "So, what's the story?"

"I like her, OK?" D said.

"I know, but what's the story?"

"I don't know. I like her."

"Is that it?"

"What else do you want? A written document that says my feelings are pure and that I want to be with her forever? That she completes me?"

Riley didn't say anything, just sat watching D for a moment.

"Look, you're not going to get that. These things don't last. I'm not going to make her believe that I want her forever when really — who knows?"

"Oh, great," Marley said. "Now I need a drink."

"Shut up, Marley," Riley said.

Riley stood up and crossed the room to stand next to D. She gave him a big hug. Riley knew him better than anyone else in the world and perhaps a little better than he knew himself.

"I think if you like her this much, you need to admit it to yourself," Riley said.

"Yeah," Brendan said, nodding before Marley elbowed him.

"I already admitted I liked her," D said.

"No, I mean you have to admit you like her and then give her the opportunity to crush you," Riley said, waving her hand in the air, dismissing it.

"Thanks, that sounds pleasant."

"D, the entire part about being in a relationship is trusting the other person enough to hurt you, to crush you, to break your heart!"

"And you know this from the whole seven months you've been dating Eric?" D yelled.

Riley stuck out her tongue.

"Nice, Ri — nice."

"I'm still right," she said.

"I just don't know."

"Well," Marley said, "you can't keep her from dating guys and meeting someone who can give her that."

"What is *that* exactly?" Brendan asked.

"D, maybe you should think about it. Like, really think about it."

"Yeah, yeah, I guess." D patted down his pockets, checking for his wallet and keys. "I think I'm going to get out of here."

"You don't want to be here when she gets back from her date?"

"No, I don't think so."

Riley nodded, Brendan pursed his lips, Marley flipped the page of her magazine.

D walked out of Riley's thinking about what she said — it didn't really make sense to him, but he *did* like Sam. He was trying to be better and trying harder to be worthy of her, so what if he wasn't ready to get close to her yet. That was really for her own good, not his.

If he got close to her and then he couldn't be the person she needed him to be, then he was really going to hurt her.

He was doing this for her own good. Perhaps, he thought, he should back off, then — because, really, for her own good, maybe she would find someone who liked her and who she liked. Someone who was worth liking.

#11 FIND SOMETHING TO DREAM ABOUT

Justin picked Sam up for their date and took her to the 92nd Street Y. For a minute Sam thought he was bringing her to exercise and felt really bad that she wore boots, but when they walked inside, Justin pulled out two tickets, handing her one.

"I bought us tickets to see this author speaking. Riley told me he was your favorite, so I thought . . ."

Sam looked at the ticket that had PETE BRYANT written across it in large letters. Her heart skipped a beat. Samantha's favorite author. Samantha's idol, and the man who stood between her and the writing program of her dreams.

"This is amazing, Justin, thank you!" she said, hugging him tightly. When she pulled back, he looked a little embarrassed but really pleased that she liked what they were doing on their date.

Pete Bryant had changed Samantha's life. Probably in a way that would be uncomfortable for him to hear, almost as uncomfortable as it would be for Samantha to explain. But the first book of Pete Bryant's that Samantha had read, *Apples & Oranges,* changed her life.

Some people can point to a family member who mentored them through adolescence, some people can point to a movie or a song that really had meaning for them and gave them the strength to do the difficult things that needed to be done. *Apples & Oranges* was all those things to Samantha.

The book, about an invisible girl who never realized she was invisible — instead believing she was just unimportant and unloved — seemed to Samantha the most important book in contemporary literature. Perhaps, if she thought about it carefully, she'd see her own feelings in that book, but just like in the book, Samantha wondered if she was just waiting around for the one person who *could* see her to come around and show her what the world really was.

And, for a long time, Samantha thought that person should be Pete Bryant. Obviously, he helped the character in *Apples & Oranges,* he could help her. In fact, he had practically written about her! But, as Samantha got older, so did Pete Bryant. And then he got married and had three small children and what started as a childhood fantasy turned into a professional crush.

But being so close to him brought back all the childhood adoration that she thought she had culled from her personality. But it was like she was a fanatical fan and she did the best she could to remain calm and try not to giggle and jump up and down as the staff worker opened the door to let the audience into the auditorium.

They headed in, Sam grabbing them seats as far in front as they could, and when Pete Bryant came out, it was like Sam only had eyes for him. He read from his recent book and then took questions from the audience. Sam was trying to figure out if she had enough guts to ask the question she really wanted to ask, and then she did. She raised her hand and Pete Bryant, *the* Pete Bryant, called on her from the small stage in the front of the auditorium.

"Red-haired young woman in the third row," he said.

. . . And she couldn't say a word. It was like her tongue was frozen or stuck to the roof of her mouth with glue. This was horrible! She was going to look like an idiot in front of Pete!

"Hi," Justin said, standing up next to Samantha, taking her elbow. "My friend here just wanted to say she was a really big fan." That drew a few chuckles from the audience and, when Samantha nodded like crazy, a chuckle from the author as well. "And she wanted to know what was the most important thing to you when you decided to become a writer."

"Great question, red-haired young woman's friend," Pete Bryant said, and the audience laughed again.

Samantha sat down, her pulse racing. Justin reached over and gave her hand a squeeze and held it there, and Sam let him.

"I always want to remain true to the experience," Pete said. "Whether I'm writing about killer unicorns or hunting in Wales, it's important to leave a little bit of yourself on the page. It's the part that feels authentic to readers. It was important to me to be able to do that, so I could connect with my readers."

And then Pete Bryant, idol of all literary idols, winked at Samantha.

And Samantha fell in love. All over again.

Samantha went home after her date with Justin because she had promised her parents that she'd spend time with them.

"I feel like we haven't even seen you since you came home," Samantha's mom said over their late dinner. Samantha's dad nodded while spooning some of Sam's mom's mashed potatoes onto his plate; he was nodding but only half paying attention. A sports game was playing in the background and he had his head swiveled around to watch while he ate. Sam's mom always threatened to turn off the television, and her father's solution was always to move the TV farther away — because, he contended, he didn't want to watch it, he only wanted to listen — but that only resulted in her father having a long stretch of his neck and food trailing over most of his shirts from his waistline to over his left shoulder. Her mother had once told her, while she was still away at school, that she had thought about moving the television into the dining room so that she wouldn't have to spend so much money getting his shirts specially laundered, but she didn't necessarily want him to "win" either.

Samantha found the entire domestic scene half comfortable, half very unusual. She still felt like New Horizons was her home and this apartment where her brother lived with her parents was a place she visited during short stretches when she couldn't stay at school.

She felt a little awkward about being answerable to her parents in a way she wasn't while she was at school, like she was always trying to remember what the rules were and when she had to ask for permission.

This hadn't been a problem at school: There was nowhere to go anyway.

But at home, she supposed, she hadn't been at home as much as she would've been expected to be.

"I'm sorry," Sam said, putting her fork down. "I didn't —"

"No, no," her mother cut her off, waving her hand in the air. "I'm glad you've got friends and a social life here. It's great."

At the phrase "social life" her younger brother started miming kissing as he made out with the back of his hand. He stopped abruptly when his mother shot him a confused look. Sam smirked. He smirked back.

"Sam's got a boyfriend. Several, actually," Andrew said, smirking some more.

Before Sam had a chance to defend herself (and denounce and then kill her brother), her mother caught him off guard. "Why should that be surprising? Sam's a beautiful young lady and of course there are boys who are interested in dating her. Isn't that right, Charles?"

Samantha's father turned back around, a glob of gravy hitting him square in the chest as he nodded. "Yes, she's quite lovely. Why — who are we talking about?"

Sam's mother sighed. "Your daughter."

"Oh, yes," Sam's father said enthusiastically. "Always felt she was quite nice, must come from good stock."

Samantha laughed and her mother rolled her eyes.

"Seriously, Charles, we're talking about Sam's boyfriends."

"Boyfriends?" Sam's father turned to look at her. Uh-oh, now they had his full attention and that was a scary thing. He wiped off his shirt, getting the small glob of gravy, all the while concentrating on her.

"Not a boyfriend, Daddy," she said, smiling.

"How many times have you been out with this boy?"

"Um, once," she said, unsure about who she was talking about — but "once" seemed like the safest answer available.

"Oh," he said, "all right, then."

"Yes," Sam continued, "we're going to the Spring Fling together."

Sam could see her father bristle. "A dance?"

165

"Oh, Charles!" her mother cried. "It's just a dance! They go to spend time together and listen to music —"

"I know what a dance is," Sam's father said stiffly. "We met at a dance." He raised an eyebrow that effectively cut off Sam's mother from whatever she was about to say, and suddenly Sam wondered what happened at the dance. And then, remembering it was her parents, she decided not to give it another thought.

"Who is this boy?" Sam's father asked.

"Um . . ." Sam's brain began churning. Who was she going to the dance with — D? Probably not. Probably she wanted to. But did he? And how about Justin? Justin was great and he probably wanted to go to the dance with her. "Justin Pembroke."

"Justin Pembroke," both of her parents repeated.

"Do you know him?" Samantha asked, praying they didn't.

"Yeah," Andrew said, snorting, "they are religious followers of the prep school social scene."

Samantha made a note that she would definitely have to beat her brother up later.

"Well, I look forward to meeting this young man," Sam's father said.

"Yeah, eventually . . ." Sam trailed off, thinking eventually she would stop talking to him, and then him meeting her parents (her father, especially) would be completely unnecessary.

"Eventually . . . before the dance," her father finished.

"What?"

166

"Before the dance, Samantha," he said, turning back toward his sports game, leaving Samantha sputtering and Sam's mother simply shrugging while she sipped her glass of wine.

Samantha was in her room, changing into her pajamas, when her mother knocked on her door.

"So, this was a good date, then?" Sam's mother asked.

"It was OK," Samantha said.

"Are you going to the dance with this boy?"

"I don't know. . . ." Samantha hesitated.

"Oh, don't mind your father, he's not nearly as bad as he sounds," Sam's mother said, a smile creeping onto her face. Sam noticed that her mom smiled like that whenever she talked about her dad. Sometimes it was gross, but right now it was kinda cute.

"No, that's not it. I just . . . well, I like this boy."

"Justin."

"D."

"I'm confused, Sam. Is this the boy you went out with tonight?"

"Noooo!" Sam said, falling onto the bed, face-first, into her pillow. "I like someone else."

"Honey, I can't understand what you're saying when you're suffocating yourself with your pillow," her mom said, pulling the pillow out from under Sam. Sam turned to face her mom.

"I like another boy, but he's not going to ask me to the dance."

"Hmm."

"And I can't ask him, because I already asked him if he wanted to hang out, and he said no, and then I asked him if he'd kiss me and he didn't say anything!"

"Oh. Um. Hmm."

"So, I don't know what to do!"

"Well," Sam's mom said, stroking the top of Sam's head gently. "I think you should go with the boy who asked you. You'll see this other boy there, won't you?"

"Maybe — what if he goes with someone else?"

"What if he does?"

Samantha shrugged.

"Go to the dance, honey. Enjoy yourself . . . and, uh, don't tell your father that you asked a boy to kiss you."

Sam laughed and sniffed a little. "OK, I won't."

"Good night, darling," Sam's mom said, standing up to leave the room. "It'll be OK, I promise."

Sam nodded as her mother turned out the light, and Sam realized that she'd just been tucked into bed. Again. But this time, she didn't mind so much.

D IS AFRAID OF SUCKING

The dance was in a week and D had been avoiding everyone, including Riley, but he had heard through the grapevine (OK, Marley had told him in the hallway — and now D was sure that Marley was some sort of sadist who simply liked to see him squirm) that Samantha would be going to the dance with Justin. It was Saturday night and D was doing something he had never done before: his homework.

He had done homework before, but not on a night when he could be out drinking and flirting and whatever else he did in the city. D was about ready to give up on his history homework, which was literally putting him to sleep while he read, when Riley texted him that she was outside.

He jumped up from his desk and ran to the elevator. When he got downstairs, Riley was waiting for him. He slowed down, took a deep breath, and walked up to her.

"Evening," he said.

He noted, with disappointment, that she was alone. And

with more disappointment that she was dressed to go out. This would be a short reprieve, apparently.

"Evening," she said, sitting on a fire hydrant that stuck out of the ground near the front wall of his building. D leaned against the wall next to her, took out a pack of cigarettes, and offered Riley one. She shook it off, so D lit one for himself and took a deep drag.

"I thought you quit smoking those," Riley said, pointing to the cigarette.

"So did I."

"So why —"

"Did you come here to lecture me?"

"Yes," Riley said, and D was sorry he asked. He took one more puff, then threw it down onto the sidewalk and stamped it out. "That's not what I was here to lecture you about."

"Think of it as a bonus," he said.

"Excellent," Riley said. "Sam's out with Justin right now."

D sighed heavily and brushed the hair back from his face. He had been happily avoiding the idea of Samantha and Justin on dates. "So the first date went well?"

"Yup," Riley said.

"And now they are out again," D said, wishing he hadn't stomped out his cigarette.

"Right," she said.

"That's great. Can I get back to my college application now?" he asked.

"You're applying to colleges?"

"Didn't I just say so?"

"Wow, don't be so testy!" Riley exclaimed. D took a deep breath and tried to relax. "And don't worry, I'll write you a recommendation, no problem."

"Just what I need," D said, then paused and looked at Riley. "I'm not doing well with this, am I?"

"Nope."

"What do I do?"

"What do you want to do?" she asked.

"I want to not want her," he said.

"That it?"

"No, I want her to stay the hell away from Justin."

"Barring that?"

"I want her to fall madly in love with me and stay home until I'm done with these stupid applications, at which point she will do and be everything I want her to be," he said. Riley snorted. The two stood up and walked out together.

"How about a reality check?" Riley asked.

"Sure, hit me."

"She likes you."

"I know that," D said. "Apparently she likes Justin too."

"She likes you more."

The two walked down the street together. Riley hooked her arm through D's and the two walked slowly, letting even the women pushing their carriages home from the market pass them.

"We are walking ridiculously slow," D said, after a woman weighed down with two bags, a dog, and a double stroller passed them, giving D and Riley a dirty look for taking up so much sidewalk when she was in a rush.

"We are enjoying each other's company."

"That we are," D said, and then after a pause, "What do you want to talk about?"

"No, I want you to talk."

"About?"

"About why you can't like her and do all the other stuff at the same time."

D thought about it for a while, a long while, as they walked. They walked past the entrance to the park and then started walking down Broadway. "It just feels like everything I do is to avoid doing the stuff I need to do, you know? I want to know that when I'm interested in her, it's because of her and not because I'm avoiding my life.

"It's not that I don't want to like her," he said slowly. "It's just that I don't *want* to like her."

"OK," Riley said, as if what he said made any sense at all.

"I'm used to girls liking me. I'm used to them pursuing me.

I'm not used to doing the pursuing. What if I pursue her and she decides she doesn't like me anymore?"

"Then I assume you will break up or whatever," Riley said.

"Exactly, and if I like her —"

"It'll suck."

"Exactly."

Riley thought for a minute and then looked D square in the eye, pulled his hands toward her, and held them there. "It sucks right now, D."

D nodded slowly, Riley matching his nods, as he thought about that. It sucked now. It would suck if Samantha didn't like him, but it would suck either way. That, of course, would suck a lot more, and he said as much.

Samantha was out on her second date with Justin and she was having fun. They went to Chelsea Piers and bowled (well, Justin bowled, Samantha gutter-bowled), so they sat in an awesome darkened bowling alley while Samantha wished she hadn't worn a skirt (but Justin was smart and thought to bring an extra pair of socks).

Justin had been really cute and had been trying really hard, so he had packed tons of food, in little baggies — and if Samantha had thought it would be fancy food, she was doomed to disappointment.

"I hope you don't mind," Justin had said, pulling out sandwiches. "I wanted to make everything myself." Samantha smiled. "Except all I know how to make is PB and J, so, um, that's what we've got here." Samantha laughed and Justin started laughing with her, only to calm down and start up again after they pulled two really sad-looking sandwiches out of their plastic baggies.

"I could only find prune spread; we were out of grape

jelly. . . ." he offered by way of explanation when she bit into her sandwich and looked up at him questioningly.

It was a good date. It was a simple date, but Justin was being overwhelmingly kind and Samantha could almost forget about D as she looked at Justin. Justin looked at her like he could be in love with her.

"I hear you do that," she said.

"Do what?"

"Look at girls like you are in love with them," Samantha said.

"Ah, yes," Justin said. "But I'm not."

"No, you're not."

"I'm not in love with you," he said slowly.

"I know that," Samantha said, just as slowly, and found it oddly reassuring that the sentiment didn't even sting.

"But I like you," he said. "I like how you talk and I like what you say. I like the way you wear your hair." Samantha patted down her hair self-consciously. "I like how unaware of how pretty you are, you are." He laughed again. "That sounded weird."

"No, no," she said, "I understand."

"Anyway, I wanted to talk to you and get to know you."

"Well, we're talking now."

"And it's good."

"Yeah."

"I'm new at this, Sam," he said. "So, take it easy on me."

"New at what?"

"Liking a girl," he said with a cautious smile. Then he offered her a cookie that was completely burned to a crisp and she laughed again, but ate it and asked for another. He looked shocked and said something about not wanting to poison her on their second date.

And then he walked her home from the subway.

"Good night, Samantha," Justin said, holding her hands and standing close.

"Good night, Justin," she said, and then Justin raised his hand to her cheek and turned her head slightly, and kissed her gently, close to her mouth but not on it. And for a second Sam was disappointed.

Until he asked to see her phone, plugged his number in, and called it.

"Now I have your number and you'll never be rid of me," he said. Sam smiled up at him and then watched him as he left, walking down the street with his hands in the front pockets of his khaki pants. He got halfway down the street before turning to smile and wave. She waved back and then went inside, feeling happy.

Moments later, she received a text, and flipping her phone open — thinking it might be an early text from Justin — saw Riley's number and the message:

D showed up late. Not happy. How was date?

Samantha thought about the date. . . . It wasn't horrible. In fact, it was just the opposite. She thought about how Justin put his arm behind her — his hand at the base of her back — in a way that felt comfortable and mature. Sam couldn't quite explain it, but she felt excited by that intimacy and wondered if he was going to kiss her.

The minute she thought that, she felt sad. She didn't really like Justin. Or she liked him, but she liked him like she liked a good friend — he was an exciting boy, and very good-looking, but there was something missing.

That said, she felt like maybe it was just in her head, maybe D was making her mind loopy. But the feelings she had for D — that automatic rush, the anticipation, the jumpiness — they just weren't there with Justin. Instead Justin made her feel comfortable, like they had known each other for weeks. And yet there was a little buzz of something, which Sam couldn't quite make out, but figured it might have to do with Justin's extreme good looks and charm. She'd wait it out, she figured, wait it out and see what happened.

When Justin called her that night, he asked her to the Spring Fling.

"I don't know," Sam said.

"Is this still about Hammond?" Samantha could hear the

frustration in his voice, and wanted it to be different. She wanted to like Justin as much as she liked D. At least that would make sense; she knew Justin liked her. She didn't even know what D was up to!

"It is," Sam admitted.

"I should never have told you that play-hard-to-get crap. Now I'll never know if you're going out with me just to get him or what."

"I went out with you because I liked you, and we had fun," Sam said.

"Well, I think we'd have fun at the dance."

Sam didn't say anything.

"Look, worse comes to worst, we go as friends and have a good time."

"Can we go as friends? Really?"

"Probably not, but I'm willing to try if you are."

Sam laughed. "That sounds like a plan, then."

D RESOLVES TO FALL IN LUST, OR DEEP-LIKE, OR HAVE A CRUSH (ON SOMEONE NOT DUMB) (AND NOT DRUNK)

It was two nights before the dance and D was going to see his father. He had called his father's secretary earlier that day and she had let him know that he would be home that evening, so D was added to his father's schedule.

Sometimes D hated the way his family was. Sometimes he loved it and couldn't imagine it any other way. This was one of the latter times.

D was supposed to be at the house at eight, so he arrived several minutes earlier because, as his father put it, "Early is on time, on time is late, late is inexcusable." There had been times when he had shown up a couple of minutes late only to be turned away because, as his father explained, he had too much to take

179

care of to rearrange his schedule for a child who couldn't get his act together.

D was admitted to the house by the butler, who asked after him and said he was glad to see him. D chatted a little before asking if his father was at home — of course he was, he was always at home for dinner.

He was in the study, doing work, when D knocked on the door.

"Come in," called a gruff voice, and D walked in. His father, looking small behind the great large oak desk, was at the other end of the narrow room. This had been D's favorite room as a child, when he had come to the States to visit his father. Most of his time was spent in London with his mother, but when she got sick and couldn't care for him any longer, he remembered his first night here — still in his coat, sitting on the leather chair facing his father's desk while his father lectured him on the duties and responsibilities he would have if he was going to live here.

If, as if it hadn't already been decided, as if D had anywhere else to go.

Ever since then, being in this room had given D the simultaneous feelings of childhood joy and teenage angst. He hated it here; he loved it here. He hated his father; he loved him.

D never quite knew how to reconcile those two emotions, but now wasn't the night for that. He wasn't sure what was going to happen that night, but he knew he wouldn't fix his entire relationship with his father that evening.

"What happened?" his father asked, looking up from his paperwork that was spread out across his desk.

"What happened?" D asked, turning around and looking behind him, then back at his father. "What do you mean?"

"Are you in trouble?"

"Uh . . ."

"If you are, tell me — we can fix it, but you have to own up to it."

"I'm not in any trouble," D said, feeling both wretched that his father always thought so ill of him — albeit, he hadn't given him many reasons to think otherwise — and slightly comforted by the fact that he was so quick to offer his help. Even when it was completely unnecessary.

"Then . . ."

"I wanted to talk to you," D said. "Without it being a lecture."

"Ha," D's father said, leaning back in the chair. "Then take a seat and tell me what you'd like to talk about."

"Actually . . ."

"Is this about a girl?" D's father said.

"I didn't get anyone pregnant," D responded.

"Who said you did?"

"I figured that was your next question."

"Absolutely not," D's father huffed. "I know you're not a complete idiot. I just think that you're here. You never come here, definitely not to talk to me. You haven't been here voluntarily since you were eleven."

"Ten."

"Ten, then. So, it must be a big deal. And if you're not about to be jailed or if you didn't join the army — you didn't, did you? — then it's about a girl."

"How do you know it's about a girl?"

"Because I did the same thing with my father when I met your mother," D's father said, his booming voice trailing off at the end. "A *man* tells his father when he meets a woman he's serious about."

"Well, that provides a bad precedent, doesn't it?" D said, awkwardly rearranging himself in the leather chair. He used to love these chairs when he was younger. Would think of them as great big ships where he had to hop from one to the other, lest he fall in the deep sea between them. Now they were just two chairs in front of a large oak desk, on a solid oak floor. No more ships.

"Not necessarily," D's father said, sounding as if he felt awkward. D always wondered why his mother and father split up so many years ago. He barely remembered them together. Just a few times when his mother was in New York, they sat in this office while his father was away and she played with him here, and let him draw at his father's desk. But more of his memories were of his father in London. Walking in the park, between his parents. Watching them watch movies. The three of them had barely been together, even before his parents split up, and then when his mother got sick — never again. But prior to then there were a few good memories that made D question what happened between his parents. He never knew when to ask or what to ask. Somehow "Why did you fall out of love with my mother?" didn't seem like a good opener.

"Well, either way."

"Yes."

"I met a girl."

D's father nodded solemnly. "Who is she?" he asked.

"She has to be somebody?" D asked, his voice raised slightly. "Is she not good enough for us already?"

"Calm down, Michael. I'm just asking after who she is."

D took a deep breath and realized that he was overreacting. He just was so tightly wound, sitting here, seeking his father's approval when all he wanted was to not need it. But he needed it. For more than just college tuition. He *wanted* it.

"Her name is Samantha Owens. Her mother is a producer of a food TV show; her father writes a column for the *Times*."

"The *Times* is a good paper."

"Yeah," D said.

"And?"

"And?"

"What's she like?"

D thought about Samantha — how to describe her — and smiled. She was a mix of different words that D couldn't begin to explain. Perhaps he should tell his father about the way they met? D smiled.

"Ah, it's like that, is it?"

"Like what?" D asked defensively.

"You love her."

"I —"

"Love her?" D's father added helpfully.

"I don't know," D answered honestly.

D's father nodded. "That's a good start. There is still a question. Let the question stand until you are sure of the answer. Until then, I hope to meet her soon — she sounds delightful."

D stared at his father incredulously. "You haven't heard anything about her."

"I can see how you feel about her. I know you've never come here to tell me about a girl before. I know that you are a good boy who doesn't need to waste his time with trashy people, and I know that deep down you know the difference. Look how loyal you and the Swain girl are to each other."

"Riley?"

"Yes, that's the one," D's father said, nodding.

"You hate Riley," D accused.

"Nothing of the sort!" D's father said. "I hardly know the girl. I think she's a bit brash and perhaps a bit too . . . colorful for my taste. But anyone who remembers to send a birthday and holiday card each year, anyone who is a loyal, good friend to my son . . ."

"Riley sends you a birthday card each year?"

"You didn't know?"

D scoffed, "What I don't know about what Riley Swain does could fill rooms of books."

D's father nodded. "She sent a beautiful letter after your mother died."

D looked shocked, so his father continued, "She said you were hurting very badly and wished you had been there with her."

"I —"

"I asked if you wanted to go back," D's father said, "but you didn't want to go. And I felt . . ."

D felt his eyes begin to swell, and his nose began to hurt, and if he wasn't careful he'd cry — right here in this old study — and he might hate himself. "Yes, well, she is loud and brash."

D's father waited a moment, then nodded. "But a nice girl."

"Samantha is a good friend of hers," D said.

D's father nodded.

"I'd like you to meet her," D said. "And . . ." D took a deep breath.

"And," he continued, "I need to tell you. I'm not going to your college. I'm going to college, but I'm applying other places. I'd like to study music and I'd like your support."

"Music?"

"I've been practicing and I made some appointments for auditions for the spring semester. I have one at Juilliard in two weeks."

"And you want to do this all on your own?"

"I need to," D said, hoping his father would understand.

"I respect that," D's dad said. "How about dinner next week?"

"I'll call your secretary," D said, "to make the arrangements."

D felt buoyant. This had gone better than he could have planned.

"Michael —" D's father said as D began to stand, ready to leave the room as quickly as he came in.

"Yes, sir?" D asked.

"Nothing," D's father said. "I'll see you next week, then."

"Yes," D said, feeling as if the formality of his good-bye was the only thing that would keep him from bursting into tears like an absolute child. He nodded once to his father before closing the door behind him, then walked out of the house — saying good-bye to his father's butler — and down the street, wondering what Samantha was doing.

#13 DRESS FOR SUCCESS

The afternoon before the dance, Samantha opted to dump the writing for the day and work on finding the most amazing dress ever. Earlier, Riley had sent her a picture of the dress she'd be wearing to the dance. Followed by seven texts and two e-mails from Riley asking if Sam thought she needed to remind Eric about proper attire and about a corsage and about . . . and then three e-mails and a harried voice mail from Eric about how Riley was driving him crazy and could Samantha please talk some sense into her before he arrived.

"I need to go shopping!" Samantha yelled down the hallway of her family's home, but nobody was home, or nobody was responding, so Sam called her mother, who told her to take her credit card and buy something as long as it "wasn't too outrageously priced."

She grabbed her jeans, threw her heels in a bag, and was heading out the door when she bumped into D on the sidewalk outside the building. Literally. Like, planted face-to-face and knocked into him, sending her bag and him to the ground.

"Oh my gosh," she cried, hurrying to help him up.

"Wow," D said, "was that as good for you as it was for me?"

Sam gave a disgusted sigh. "Probably not."

"You're headed out," D said, noting the bag and the multiple pairs of shoes. "You're not pulling a Riley Swain and wearing multiple shoes today, are you?"

"No," Sam said, stuffing the shoe that D was holding out to her back in her bag. "I'm going dress shopping — these are my trial shoes."

"Dress shopping?"

"Yes, for the dance . . ."

"The dance that is tomorrow?" D asked, looking seriously confused.

"Yup, that's the one."

"And you don't have a dress yet?"

"Don't pressure me!"

D put his arm around her and rubbed her back. "Relax, this isn't bad, this is fixable."

Samantha immediately relaxed under the weight of his arm and shifted into his side, then sniffed, "It is?"

"Of course," D said, cracking his knuckles and rolling up his sleeves. "Do you have funds?"

Samantha pulled her mother's credit card out of her back pocket.

"Perfect," D said. "You've got the shoes, how about the jewelry?"

"Jewelry?" Sam asked. D sighed softly and Sam cried out, "I should just stay home — I'm unfit for dances!"

"Don't be ridiculous," D said, grabbing her hand and tucking it under his arm, pulling her down the street. "We'll start with the dress and accessorize from there."

"We?"

"Of course," D said, "unless you want to handle this one alone?"

"No, no, I need as much help as I can get," she said, but when D turned to face forward, she took a second to study his face and smiled. He really was quite beautiful. He had such blue eyes that were framed by thick dark lashes — making them seem even more amazing than they already were. He was too good-looking for her. Definitely.

"What are you thinking about?" he asked, looking at her through the corner of his eye.

"I was just thinking about how beautiful you are," Sam said.

"Beautiful? Beautiful is for women."

"Cute, then."

"Cute is for puppies and small children."

"How about handsome?"

"I'll take handsome if you say 'beyond any reasonable standard of perfection,'" he said with a smile.

"Don't go too far," she said.

He scoffed and elbowed her gently in the side and, while she was pretending he had mortally wounded her, he squeezed her against his side, the two of them stumbling down the street together.

"Let's grab a tea before you go on your shopping marathon," D said.

"I only have eighteen hours!" Sam said, checking her watch, but at D's pouting face, she acquiesced.

They found the nearest Starbucks and Sam hounded tables while D went and ordered them both tea. He carried it back to the table, handing one over to her, and then pulled fourteen Splendas out of his pocket.

Sam smiled and grabbed one.

"So, you're going to the dance, huh?"

"Uh-huh," she said. "You?"

"It depends."

"On?"

"Well, on whether or not you're going to be there."

Sam looked at him but didn't say anything. But her knees went a little mushy.

"I'm auditioning for Juilliard this weekend," he said flatly.

"Oh, wow, D, that's huge! I'm so excited for you," Sam cried.

"I mean, it's not really a big deal. My mom went there," D said. "So . . . you know."

"It's absolutely a big deal," Sam said. "Do you miss her a lot?"

"Every day."

Sam just nodded and then reached across the table and took D's hand.

"But who knows, right?" D said. "I might be just another talentless hack."

"Not from what I hear from Riley," Sam said, taking a sip of her tea.

"Riley . . ." D started, thinking about what his father said about her earlier. "Riley is different. She's always been different."

Sam was quiet for a second and then asked the question she didn't really want the answer to. "I remember when I first met her, she was kind of in love with you."

"She thought she was, but then she met Eric," D clarified.

"That's right . . . but . . . did you . . . ?"

"Did I love her?"

"Yeah," Sam said.

"Yeah, I did. I do," D said. "She's my best friend, I can't imagine life without her."

Sam nodded, and for some reason, his answer was perfect. Not at all what she was expecting, but she wasn't even sure what she had expected.

"I don't think I've ever felt about anyone the way I feel about you, though," he said, causing Sam to sputter in her tea a little.

"What?"

D just looked at her. "I just . . ." He paused. "I like you. I really like you and I worry about what you think about me and I want you to like me and I want to be so great that you can't pass me by."

Sam watched him for a moment, and then he started talking again.

"But I mean, that's silly. . . ." he said.

"No," she said. "That's not silly."

"I just wish that . . ."

"Hmm?" she asked, trying to get her pulse to calm down a little.

"I just wish I was the one taking you to this dance. I wish I was the one who had the guts to ask you and to be the one who spent all night dancing with you."

Samantha didn't know what to say. She wanted to tell him that she felt the same way, that she wanted nothing more than what he just proposed. And yet that wasn't really fair to Justin, whom she had said she was going to the dance with.

That night Sam went home and pulled out her laptop. She began typing, the words just flowing from her as she wrote a story about a girl who wanted to do all sorts of things she had never done before and a boy who wanted to stop doing all sorts of things he had done before. When she was done, she was so excited that she texted D that she wanted to celebrate and he said he'd be there in no time.

They stood outside (and Samantha was sure that her parents only looked out the window half a dozen times, and she was impressed with their restraint). She was nervous when he said he was coming over. It was late at night and they had just seen each other and she didn't know what any of it meant. But once he was there, the nervousness changed a little. It was like it seeped into every cell in her being. Her body felt like it was positively buzzing.

"I finished my sample, I think. I mean, not at all. I need to write a lot more, but I think I figured out what to write about," Sam gushed.

"That's great, Sam. I'm really proud of you."

"Proud of me?"

"Yeah, I mean, I'm proud of you for not giving up. You're an inspiration," D said, and the two looked out onto the street as an old man walked by with a little old dog. "I'm not really sure how this all works, you know."

Sam nodded. She was confused.

D was confused too; Sam could see it on his face. He pulled back and looked awkwardly at her and then smiled a self-deprecating smile and let her hands drop. He went to take a step back, but instead Sam — without thinking — stepped into him, held him by the shoulders, and with one hand, pulled his face down to hers and kissed him.

Sam kissed him.

On the lips.

Over and over again.

And whatever nervousness she felt had changed. She was happy to be there, happy when his strong arms went around her and pulled her against him. Happy to feel the way his hand went into the hair at the nape of her neck, while squeezing her gently so she felt like she was wrapped inside of him.

And the kiss.

Boy, could he kiss.

It was the best kiss she ever had. And she had kissed him. Sam was still surprised, but now he was kissing her back — and there was an urgency to it, like he had been waiting and wanting to do this for a long time and finally the chance arose and he wasn't going to stop for anything.

Sam loved him.

It struck her, as simple as that, as quickly as that.

She loved him.

D walked home feeling buoyant. He had kissed her.

Well, she had kissed him, if you wanted to be technical about it — but it didn't matter, there was kissing! He jumped up and down on the sidewalk, causing an old lady to gasp in shock. He apologized, "She kissed me." And then smiled at her.

The old lady gave him a very dirty look.

But he didn't care, because Sam kissed him. And he kissed her. And he kept kissing her until it was too late to keep kissing her and until he felt like his entire body was wrapped up in the idea and feelings of kissing her.

He loved kissing her.

He loved kissing Samantha Owens.

He loved her.

That thought stopped D short. He loved her? Could he love her? He barely knew her really . . . a few weeks, a month, or more? One kiss. Or rather, an hour of one kiss. And he loved her? It wasn't possible.

He needed to think.

He needed to go to this dance, which he hadn't been planning on going to at all — Michael D. Hammond III at a school dance? Inconceivable. But when Samantha asked if he was going, he automatically said yes. She had looked so sweet when she had asked if he'd dance with her.

And when — in his head — he answered, *I would dance every single dance — even though I can't dance at all — if only to have an excuse to touch you*, he stopped and thought about how Justin was probably thinking the same thing. Which is why he had said that to her, and he had seen her disappointment and felt good about it — because that's how he felt. Disappointed that she was going with someone else to the stupid dance that he was now dying to go to.

But it was his fault for not asking her. Although he supposed she could have asked him. It didn't matter now. They had kissed.

But maybe it did matter. Maybe Samantha would be sitting at home thinking he was a jerk for kissing her when she had another date to the dance. Maybe this made it weird and she'd resent the weirdness.

D wanted to stop thinking about this. Crap — was this what women went through? *Good luck to them*, he thought. He needed to go do something guy-ish. Like yell at the television or start a fire. Whatever, he knew that he'd probably just go home, sit on his couch, stare at the ceiling, and think about kissing Samantha Owens.

It was all he wanted to do.

D felt pathetic.

#14 GO TO A SCHOOL DANCE

The next night Samantha was just finished getting dressed when her brother knocked on her door. She called for him to come in, and he did a low whistle when he saw her.

"Nice dress," he said.

She smoothed down the front of the black dress with hand-sewn embroidery of dark red flowers along the bottom and over the bodice that was tight against her chest. She covered her bare shoulders with a short shawl. She'd freeze tonight, but it would be worth it. She couldn't help wonder about what D would think when he saw her. Would he be thinking about their kiss as much as she had?

"Thanks, Andrew," she said. "I really like it."

"How much did it cost?"

"Didn't anyone ever tell you it was rude to ask that?"

"Sure, how much did it cost?"

"Too much, that's all you're getting out of me," she said, smiling.

"Well, you look awesome."

"Aw, thanks, honey," she said. "That's so sweet of you!" She grabbed her younger brother and gave him a big bear hug while he squirmed to get away.

"Gah!" he yelled, escaping her clutches while he smoothed his hair down. "Have fun at the dance!"

"'K!" she called after him as he escaped, letting Riley in at the same time. Riley was wearing a pink and white polka-dotted dress that looked like it was made in the 1950s.

"OMG!" Riley squealed. "You look gorgi!"

Samantha laughed. "Thanks, you look pretty gorgi yourself."

Samantha's brother and father ran for cover the minute the squealing began, but Sam's mother broke out the camera and made the girls pose for several pictures until Andrew called upstairs that their dates were waiting.

"They're here?" Sam started darting around the room, looking for her bag and grabbing things that she might need that night.

"Whoa there, cowgirl, calm down, we have time."

"What, we just leave them down there waiting?"

"Exactly," Riley said, bouncing into her seat on Sam's bed. Sam watched her for a second before shrugging and perching on the bed next to her.

"We look awesome," Riley said. "I'm not just saying that because it's us — I'm saying it because it is true."

"I believe you."

"We're going to have fun tonight." And then Riley gave her friend a hug.

The two girls went downstairs, where Eric was sitting in a not-quite-suit, but he still looked very handsome anyway. It was a nice reunion for Sam and Eric, who hadn't seen each other since Sam left New Horizons. And Justin was sitting talking to Samantha's father — Justin looked way more comfortable than Sam's father did. But he was attempting to do his fatherly duties, asking who was driving (they would take a cab) and who was drinking (no one raised their hands, except Andrew — which got him a smack upside the head), and then they were leaving.

Sam's father held her back from the group as the others made their way out the door. "I still expect to meet him before your first big date," he said to her.

"Huh?" Sam asked, looking at Justin, who had turned around to smile at her down the steps.

"No, not that one. The one that you were all loopy about the other day."

"How do you know he's not the one who I'm all loopy about?"

"A father knows these things," he said gruffly, while she laughed and kissed his cheek, saying that he would definitely meet him.

She walked out the front door, her parents and her younger brother in the door frame waving her away. She followed Eric, Riley, and Justin down the steps to the car that Riley had called to take them to the dance at the school.

Samantha was excited, knowing she'd be seeing D there.

And when Justin leaned over and told her how beautiful she looked, she thanked him, but couldn't stop thinking about what D would think when he saw her.

D ATTENDS MORE SCHOOL-SANCTIONED FUNCTIONS

D hated school dances. Hated them. Wished them to the devil.

He stood in the center of the room, getting jostled by underclassmen who didn't know better than to walk around him and give him a wide berth. He saw a few stares in his direction and realized that this was definitely not his normal scene . . . but it didn't matter, he was here to see Samantha, even if it was only for one dance. He was going to hold her and dance with her and make an idiot of himself on the dance floor and it was going to be perfect.

"Hammond," Justin said behind him, clapping him on the back.

D turned around and immediately searched for Samantha.

"She's in the bathroom with Riley," Justin said, straightening his collar. "Girls — they need so much upkeep."

D nodded distractedly, unsure of what to say to Justin now

that they were sort of after the same girl. But D knew he'd win. At least he was pretty sure.

"So, you're out to steal my date, huh?"

"Um . . ."

"I figured. I saw the way you two looked at each other, even early on," Justin said, shrugging it off.

"You saw?"

"Saw . . . ?"

"You saw that I liked her?" D asked.

"Yeah, a blind man could've seen that, Hammond. Get with it."

"And you asked her out anyway?"

"Of course I did," Justin said.

"Why the hell for?" D could barely keep from yelling.

"Kimberly Penington."

"Who?"

"Kimberly Penington. Seventh grade, blond hair, moved here from Australia and then moved back the next semester."

"Yeah? I vaguely remember her — what does that have to do with anything?"

"You kissed her."

"Justin, I've kissed a lot of girls."

"Well, I really liked that one, and you kissed her first."

"What does that have to do with anything?" D said, getting the sneaking suspicion he wouldn't like what was coming next.

"Well, you really liked Samantha and *I* kissed her first," Justin said. "Oddly, though, I really like her — so if you are thinking of screwing it up, just let me know. I don't mind being the last one to kiss her too."

"You're a jerk," D said.

"Yeah, but I'm the jerk that is with Sam," Justin said. D looked at him to gauge if he was serious or not; he was, D decided, and he sighed. "Plus, she told me we were only here as friends anyway."

D smiled. "Sorry I kissed your girl."

"Don't worry about it, we're even."

D ground his teeth and tried to smile.

"Holy crap, Hammond. Relax, it was a kiss. I don't think she was even that into it."

D could barely see straight.

"Really like this one, eh?" Justin asked. "What are you going to do?"

D tried not to say anything, lest Justin decide he wasn't willing to give up his date after all, but Justin just laughed and said, "Don't screw it up," and walked away.

D watched as he approached Marley, who looked bored as usual but agreed to dance with him.

That kid, D thought, was such a weirdo.

#15 FIND THE RIGHT GUY

Samantha looked around and in the middle of the dance floor, directly in front of her, was D. Standing alone, in a serious suit that made him look especially gorgeous.

You look gorgeous, she thought.

He smiled at her and she walked toward him.

"You look gorgeous," he said.

"I was just thinking the same thing about you."

"It's mutual admiration, then," D said. "Uh, where's your date?"

"Dancing with Marley."

"Well, I'm not here with anyone. If you're desperate, I'd be happy to dance with you."

"Desperate?"

"For a partner, I mean," D said, smiling.

"You're not scared of dancing, is that it?"

"Scared, no."

"No?"

"Terrified maybe; scared is a little weak."

"Well, maybe then we should sit down. . . ."

D pulled her back by the hand and leaned over her, whispering in her ear, "I want to dance with you. Slow dance, even. Just so I can be near you."

She smiled, his breath brushing against her ear, and a shiver went up her spine and raised the gooseflesh on her arms.

"Let's find a place to sit, until the music begins?" D asked.

"Yes, definitely," she said, following him to the table where Riley and Eric were sitting and cuddling up to each other.

"You know . . . my dad wants to meet you," D said.

"Funny, my dad wants to meet you too."

"Ugh, let's do your dad first."

"My dad is a teddy bear!"

"No man is a teddy bear when it comes to the boy in love with his little girl."

Sam watched him and then broke into a huge smile. She didn't say a word, but stood up, standing between his legs as he sat in his chair, and bent over him, him having to tilt his head back to look at her. She kissed him. Lightly at first and then again and again and again — well, at least until one of the teacher chaperones came by and tapped her on the shoulder, shaking her head.

"Mrs. Donnegan! She was taking advantage of me, thank you for being so vigilant!" D called after the teacher.

The teacher coughed, while Sam hit him on the shoulder.

"I would never believe such a thing, Mr. Hammond," Mrs. Donnegan responded.

Sam laughed, and then the music started.

"Dance with me?" she asked.

"Of course," he said, letting her pull him onto the dance floor.

He wrapped his arms around her, and they rocked back and forth together, her head against his shoulder and his arms around her.

"Your hair smells pretty," he said.

"Thanks," she replied.

"What are you thinking about?" he asked.

"Kissing you again."

"Good."

"Good?"

"Yes, good."

"What are you thinking about?"

"Italian soccer," he said, earning himself a whack on the arm. He laughed at her distress.

"I'm thinking that I want to know if you'll go with me to prom."

Sam tilted her head, and looked at him. "That is months away."

"Well, I can't take the risk that another guy will ask you first," D said, motioning his head toward Justin, who was watching them and smirking.

Sam looked from Justin to D, who was watching her intently. "So," he said, "Um . . . will you?"

He looked so charmingly ill at ease that Sam had to smile and put him out of his misery. "Of course," she said, and then she wrapped her hands around his neck, and pulled him down into a kiss.

CREATIVE WRITING PROGRAM
UNIVERSITY OF CALIFORNIA,
LOS ANGELES

Dear Samantha,

    Thank you for sending along this new sample. I'm impressed with the progress you've made. Reading this sample, I finally feel like I got to know a little bit about Samantha Owens the person and not just Samantha Owens the writer.

    I'd like to see you as part of next year's class — so we're offering you admission into the writing program starting in the Spring.

                          Sincerely,
                          Pete Bryant

AUTHOR'S NOTE

Dear reader,

A quick confession — I don't know Latin and I can't write haiku. So I'd like to (publicly) thank Google (for researching Latin phrases) and Sam (for helping me with Walker's trombone haiku).

x Nina Beck